DANGER'S VICE

A HOLLY DANGER NOVEL:
BOOK TWO

AMANDA CARLSON

DANGER'S VICE

A HOLLY DANGER NOVEL: BOOK TWO

Copyright © 2017 Amanda Carlson, Inc.

ISBN: 978-1-944431-18-1

OTHER BOOKS BY AMANDA CARLSON

Jessica McClain Series:
Urban Fantasy
BLOODED
FULL BLOODED
HOT BLOODED
COLD BLOODED
RED BLOODED
PURE BLOODED
BLUE BLOODED

Sin City Collectors:
Paranormal Romance
ACES WILD
ANTE UP
ALL IN

Phoebe Meadows:
Contemporary Fantasy
STRUCK
FREED
EXILED

Holly Danger:
Futuristic Dystopian
DANGER'S HALO
DANGER'S VICE
DANGER'S RACE
DANGER'S CURE
DANGER'S HUNT
DANGER'S FATE

For Dad. I love you.

Chapter 1

"What do you mean she's in holding?" I paced in front of the worktable where Lockland sat, fingers pressed to his temples like he was trying to push back a headache. That made two of us. "What the hell is *holding* anyway?" I braced my fists on top of the cool metal, leaning over so I could get my answer up close and personal.

I was tired. Sleep had been evasive at best. Daze had almost died the night before, so I'd been up on and off, never really settling into any good REM.

But the kid was better, so that was a plus.

I'd arrived in Port Station this morning to pick up my craft, only to find her missing. She'd been parked in a hard-to-reach location—like, on-top-of-a-building hard to reach.

"I'm working on it." Lockland raised his head. Smudges darkened the skin underneath his eyes, indicating he hadn't slept all that well either. "The guards brought her in."

The table in Bender's workshop that I was hovering over was covered in junk. Pixie motors, dirty rags, random fittings, and for the first time, I noticed some distinctly shaped items of the personal pleasure variety.

I stood, raising a single eyebrow.

Doing my best to ignore the assortment of colorful and unnaturally glossy toys, I made my way over to a nearby chair and sat. I sighed. "Where did they take her?" I tried to brush my hair away from my face, but my fingers got hooked in the uncooperative mess, which fell around my shoulders in thick, ropy strands, saturated with sweat and who knew what else. A trip to a cleaning stall was high on my to-do list. After everything else. "And how did they achieve that? She was on top of a fucking building. At an angle."

"They have a mover drone," Lockland replied. Along with the half-moons shadowing his lower lids, the jet-black stubble tracing his currently clenched jaw was longer than usual, and his short hair was in need of a trim. Seeing Lockland unkempt was unusual, as the man took it to heart to stay kempt, but I understood why. None of us had had time to do anything other than survive the last few days. "Like people used before the dark days to transport large objects like floating craft and construction bots."

"Yeah, I know what a mover drone is. Thanks for that." I stood, irked that we'd found ourselves in this predicament. It'd been a lot of years since anyone had gotten the best of us. We were a solid team, working as a single unit, with the number-one priority being keeping each other alive. It was the only way to survive in this city. We each had a talent. Mine was salvaging and positioning my ear to the ground, making sure nobody messed with us, and if they did, they paid for it.

I'd failed big-time and I'd missed something huge.

Outskirts had descended into town two months prior with plans to take over the city. It was unacceptable that we hadn't had any intel before last week. The only saving grace was that I'd made their leader pay by searing a hole through his chest, almost losing my life in the process. I had zero regrets. I'd do it again in a heartbeat.

I wandered toward the large graphene wall that separated us from the outside, my boots clacking over the chipped mezzanine floor. Bender's shop was enormous. It used to house retail space before disaster struck, back when industry had thrived. Instead of like now, when making do by salvaging and repairing whatever the hell you could find was all we had.

Resting a shoulder against one of the massive pillars, I crossed my arms. "There's something extremely valuable stored inside Luce"—my head bobbed between Lockland and Bender, who sat on his usual stool, stationed close to the cooling unit—"and it's imperative we get her back as soon as possible."

The quantum drive that Daze, my new sustainee, had stolen from Tandor, the zealot freak who'd threatened to take over the government, was tucked away inside a secret compartment under my craft's dash. We had no idea what was on it, but whatever data it contained, it was important. The odds that the guards in Port Station had discovered it were iffy, but they existed. My hidey-holes were secure, but a pro would find it eventually.

"We'll get her back," Bender said gruffly as he stood.

"I sure as hell hope so," I said, my frustration leaking through my words like a gas canister with a puncture. "Any word on Darby's location?" Our friend and resident tech wizard-slash-scientist had been detained by the government. We'd had very little news thus far, which was concerning.

"No," Lockland answered. "Claire has been unresponsive."

"Since when?" I dropped my arms, my burgeoning headache forgotten in an instant.

"Late last night."

Bender grabbed a large box off a shelf and brought it over to a worktable, where he began rummaging inside for something, his biceps straining as he moved. Bender was one of the most intimidating presences in the dark city. His shiny, bald dome gleamed without a speck of hair, and his muscles were corded and well defined. He stood a head taller than most and used that height to his advantage. "That's not like her," he grumbled, his face aimed inside the box, his hands shifting things around. "Something has to be wrong."

"I couldn't agree more," I said, watching what he was doing. "She always picks up." I addressed Lockland. "What did she say when you last spoke with her?"

"The conversation was a little strange," Lockland admitted, joining us. "She sounded distant and hurried."

"Distant how?" I plucked up the object Bender had just set on the table and turned it over in my hand. It resembled a hydro-bomb, but it had a hard, bumpy coating. "You were on a tech phone. How could she sound distant?" I glanced at Bender. "What the hell are these things?" It sat heavy in my palm. Bombs were light, usually made of compressed, highly flammable gas.

Bender grinned. "It's a fuel rocket. I remembered I had these once we came back from dealing with that asshole Tandor. They would've come in handy."

I examined the new toy. "These are what I'd call back-in-the-day bombs, but they give a nice directional blast, from what I've heard. I've never used one." The top of the oval was weaker than the rest of the body. It was meant to break first, localizing the direction of the explosion. I met Lockland's gaze across the table. His mouth turned down in a frown as I continued to manhandle the fuel rocket. "What? These things have a tough skin, and the activation switch is tucked inside a false bottom." I slid my thumb over the rough exterior to prove my point. "It's not going to break in my hand." He said nothing, but he continued to judge the situation with his eyes, like a father would a child's naughty behavior. I set the bomb down carefully and huffed, crossing my arms. "Fine. You haven't finished telling us why Claire sounded distant. Please continue."

"I'm not sure," Lockland said. "It's possible there was frequency interference, but I didn't hear any of the telltale breaks. She just sounded far away. She said the government was still holding Darby in one of the main cells, but they'd be moving him soon and she'd let us know. That was it."

Once all the bombs had been unpacked, Bender transferred them one by one to a battered but sturdy carrying case with a cushy chemi-foam interior, no doubt to load them into his craft so he'd have them on hand from now on. Bender flew a G5 dronecraft, which was known for its stability and reinforced frame, making it one of the most durable crafts ever made. It was parked on the roof of this building in a protected slot. If you messed with his craft, Bender would find you, and everyone in all the neighborhoods knew it.

"If the government gave Darby Babble, like Tandor did, to weasel information out of him," Bender growled, "he likely ratted us out, including Claire. She was probably in a hurry to get to a safe place."

I shook my head. "I don't think so. I heard months ago that the government ran out of Babble." Babble was an injectable truth serum developed well before the dark days. Once given a dose, you were compelled to answer any question truthfully, in full, glaring detail, and you remembered zilch when you woke. "I have no idea how Tandor got his hands on it, but if Claire was in the process of running, it had to be because of something else." I thought about it. "Maybe she wasn't actually *fleeing*. She could've been distracted. She's working hard to help Darby, and you know how she gets." Claire had been a stabilizing force in my life from age nine on and, in my opinion, was stronger than all of us put together. Multitasking was an artform to her, but juggling so many things would wear anyone out eventually. "If I know anything about Claire, it's that she's trying to get Darby out of government hands, all while sacrificing her well-being and everything else along with it. She'll do whatever it takes, however long it takes." How Darby got snatched by the government was still a mystery. Last we'd heard, Tandor and his group had him, after luring Darby into their snare by convincing him he was working on a cure to Plush addiction.

Instead, Tandor had given him Babble, so he could infiltrate our crew.

It'd worked, and the zealot had been able to track us down. Everything had exploded in our faces soon after.

Plush was a powerful pharma-psychotic drug that flooded the brain with endorphins, blissing out whoever took it to unfathomable heights. The only problem was, one dose left you completely addicted and permanently altered. We called the addicts pleasure seekers—seekers, for short. The more of the toxic cocktail they ingested, the more their body chemistry changed, making them wildly aggressive and hazardous to everyone's health. Dying at the hands of a seeker was death by mutilation. Not a pretty way to go.

It was widely speculated that the government had provided seekers with a steady stream of Plush to keep them in check, even before the dark days, though it had never been confirmed.

But seekers had to have been getting their fix from someplace. They certainly weren't making it themselves.

Lockland poured himself a cup of water from a jug on the counter. Water was something we had in abundance around here since it rained twenty-four seven. The rare day that the city went without precip was considered a holiday—but only if you liked celebrating things by donning a face mask so you didn't inhale a lungful of iron dust. The particles in the air increased when the droplets of rain didn't encase them and carry them safely to the ground. Because of the constant iron-rich environment, everything around here was stained a lovely rust color.

"I agree. Claire will do whatever it takes to get Darby out," Lockland said between sips. "She could've been in a hurry. It might not have anything to do with his situation. I refuse to leap to any conclusions at the moment. We'll give her another half a day to get a hold of us before we act. Until then, we sit tight."

"How's the kid?" Bender carried the container of fuel rockets over to a door that led to a hallway, which in turn led to Bender's private quarters, as well as the roof.

My new sustainee, Daze, had suffered greatly under Tandor. He'd been captured as a street kid and forced to lie to me to stay alive, all while trying to protect his friend. But he'd double-crossed Tandor in the end, almost sacrificing his life for ours.

I'd decided to forgive him.

"Without the medi-pod at the barracks, he would've died." I walked over to the counter and leaned against it. I'd ended up flying Case's Q7 to his safe place by the sea after we'd defeated Tandor. If we hadn't made it in time, Daze would've succumbed to his injuries. "We're staying at the bunker for another week for ongoing treatments. But the kid is scrappy. He'll be fine. He wanted to come today, but I told him no. He needs a few more days before he's fully mobile. But, just so you know, he's sorry. He'll tell you in person when he gets a chance."

Lockland opened the cooling unit next to me and set the water inside. "What about this Case guy? Is he militia? Or an outskirt?" His gaze landed firmly on mine, his eyes intent as he closed the door. "He played a part in saving the kid and provided more than a distraction at the gorge, but there are questions that need answering. Tandor and his crew knew where to find us yesterday. They picked us up within hours. Nobody knew our plans, except the three of us." He nodded between Bender and me as he positioned himself less than a meter away, crossing his arms, his legs splayed. It was his *don't fuck with me* pose, and it was highly effective.

It was time to come clean.

I bowed my head. This was a tricky story to tell. Tandor and his men had known our movements because Case had placed a tracker inside me—between the first and middle fingers on my right hand—and had been feeding them information, playing both sides.

At the time, it'd made us enemies.

In retaliation, I'd drugged him with a tranq dart rammed none-too-gently into his thigh. It should've knocked him out for much longer, but he'd somehow fought through the effects and ended up providing the distraction we needed to defeat Tandor, as well as taking out a number of Tandor's men with his craft. Then he'd helped me get Daze back to safety, to the only nongovernmental medi-pod I knew existed anywhere.

In my eyes, that made him neutral.

Neither ally, nor adversary.

But I wasn't sure how the guys would see it. I lifted my head and cleared my throat. "He hasn't confirmed if he's militia or not, but the barracks certainly are, and he has access." To say Case wasn't chatty was an understatement. If the man had said more than five words to me this morning on our trip to Port Station to get Luce, I hadn't heard them. "And the reason Tandor was able to find us was because Case injected me with a tracker. He sedated me while I was sleeping, the night Daze was taken and we went back to the bunker." I let that sink in. "That's the reason I knocked him out and came to the gorge myself." I shrugged. "He was playing both sides to get revenge for his nephew. His sustainee sister was one of Tandor's followers, and she killed her son at the zealot's request. In my estimation, after everything that's gone down, he's neutral. But I'll go with whatever. Daze needs that medi-pod for at least a week." I shoved away from the counter. "After that, I'm happy to send Case packing."

They were both quiet for a moment. "I only need to know one thing." Bender's tone was like steel. "Can we trust him?"

That same thought was on my mind.

How well can you trust someone who's continually played you? "Like I said, he's neutral. He has no skin in our game anymore. My guess is we won't need to trust him, because he'll head back to wherever he came from soon enough." I stopped in front of the worktable, my eyes inadvertently landing once again on the colorful array of conical-shaped sex toys. They ranged from big to bigger, with connection points integrated into the tops, so the user could choose to go virtual in tandem if they so desired. "Jesus, Bender, when did you start fixing everything under our nonexistent sun?"

Bender grunted, glancing over my shoulder to see what I was talking about. "Just pulled those out of storage. They were from a salvage a few years back. Forgot all about 'em. They came from that old licensed Pleasure Emporium near the canals." I knew exactly where that was. I'd searched there a few times for useful tidbits over the years, but had never come across anything like this. They were in too good of condition to have been left out in the open. "I found them shoved into a wall I happened to bash in with my macro-sledge." He pinned me with a look, his mouth quirking up on one side. Catching Bender in a real smile was next to impossible. "Didn't take you as an antistimulus gal." An actual snicker came out. "They each came with a pair of coded VR goggles, though the trigger nodules are missing, which is a damn shame. But they'll bring in some real coin. That is, if I have enough pixie motors to fix 'em up. They're in rough shape on the inside, but their synthetic covering is damn near lifelike, even after all these years. Go ahead, touch one." He gave me a shit-eating grin. I barely refrained from sticking out my tongue like a six-year-old and then following it up with a punch to the face to get rid of that manic smile.

"I'm not anti-anything," I grumbled, stuffing my hands in my pockets. There was no way I was going to touch those things. "And there's nothing lifelike about them. Human skin doesn't come in neon purple or nuclear orange, nor does it have a sheen." I gave him the stink-eye, daring him to form a rebuttal as I maneuvered away.

If anyone had bothered to ask me, some things didn't *require* batteries, nodes, and goggles.

But toys like these were the norm before the dark days. Sexual satisfaction had been a booming, multitrillion-dollar industry, according to the historical data left behind. You could purchase sex in every shape and form—from a TrueLife bot, to a hologram program with sensory nodules, and for the big bucks, even a human. And from what I'd read, any combination of the three.

The industry had been heavily regulated by the government, the biggest seller being the "total" virtual experience. A pleasure-seeking patron booked a room at a licensed emporium—just like the one where Bender had found his loot—selected their choice du jour, and away they went.

Plush had been developed as a "monitored" enhancing substance to go along with these pleasurable experiences. According to the old ads left behind, it was to be ingested to "unleash the complete sensory fantasy." A few aluminum mega-boards had endured the test of time, mostly in the zoom tunnels, where people had traversed the city daily on briskly moving platforms that transported them through underground corridors filled with visual distractions. The tunnels between the mag-lev stations were the perfect places to reach a large audience, as daily riders swelled into the millions.

Inside the tubes themselves, which crisscrossed the city and beyond, were both screen and hologram advertisements, and companies hadn't held back. Every gap of space had been utilized.

The mega-boards I'd seen for myself had the company's name, Bliss Corp, engraved along the bottom and the word *Plush* front and center in huge seductive script, along with an etching of a heavily augmented woman holding a bullet-shaped vial cradled in her open palm.

In addition to the boards, which had been the only things to weather damage and time, Bliss Corp's live screen and hologram ads had been legendary, constantly pushing the boundaries of what could be shown in public. Since it was literally a multitrillion-dollar industry, no one was going to stop them.

According to public records, just months prior to the dark days, something had gone awry with Plush. People were getting sick, exhibiting serious anger and control issues. The little rainbow-colored pill had recently gone through an overhaul, to both keep up with demand and address the fact that pleasure seekers were requiring larger and larger doses to achieve the same stimulus effect they'd initially received. Bliss Corp had partnered with SensiTouch to come up with a "new and improved" formula—marketed still as Plush, but with "enhanced capabilities." It had hit the market less than six months before disaster struck.

Those "enhancements" had caused irreversible damage, but before they could fix the formula, a meteor the size of a mountain had destroyed life as every single soul on the planet had known it. Glancing off the moon, it had broken into three pieces, striking Earth with enough force to obliterate anything within thousands of kilometers of each blast and sending enough dirt, rocks, and debris up into the upper atmosphere to congest the sky for decades to come.

Bender chuckled, bringing me back to the here and now.

He was gleeful at my obvious discomfort as he hauled open the door to the cooling unit. "When you're talking about pleasure," he growled, "color doesn't matter in the least. Purple, orange, green, they achieve the same desired out*come*." He upended a jug of aminos, taking large swigs. Once he was done, he ran a forearm over his mouth, continuing to grin hard enough to show teeth. "I'll be sure to save you one."

I made a noise between a squeak and a gurgle, but was saved from having to reply as Lockland cleared his throat. "We've got more important things to discuss than pleasure toys. First on the agenda is getting Luce back and procuring that quantum drive. The data on it was integral to Tandor's plans, and we need it in our possession before any survivors from his group—if there are any—track it down. We do it tonight at blackout. I'll be in touch with my contacts in Port Station today. If they don't choose to release Luce, we'll go in and take her."

I nodded. "Sounds good." I patted the Gem at my waist. My laser gun had seared a solid hole through Tandor yesterday. I'd smoked him, according to Daze. I was ready to get Luce back, whatever it took.

"Do you happen to have any reflective cloth lying around?" Lockland asked as he began to pace. "I had some, but used the last bit recently. It could come in handy tonight."

"I think so." Going back to my residence in the

canals would be unadvisable, not knowing what Darby had told the outskirts or the government. I'd recently taken him there and introduced him to my fortress of illegal objects—including fifty times the amount of allowable solar panels, a cache of batteries that would qualify me for a nice over-the-head acid bath, and an E-unit that made compressed hydrogen bombs and cubes, which was so illegal they wouldn't even come searching for it, because no one in their right mind would be stupid enough to have one. "My residence in The North has a stockpile of stuff. I haven't been through it in a while, but I can go there today."

"Good," he said. "Do you need a lift?"

I shook my head. "No. I need to hit one of my stashes on the way, so I'll head there on foot." There was a certain item I needed. It was extremely rare. A sneaky kind of deadly. Not knowing what was in store for us moving forward, I knew it would be better to be armed and prepared with one of my biggest assets until the threat of danger passed. But, honestly, it never really went away. As my last name suggested, Danger was everywhere.

"Fine. We meet back here an hour before blackout." During blackout, the city shut down to conserve on battery power and to try to minimize chaos for its few remaining residents. But lots of crazy stuff happened after dark. "And, Holly"—I turned at the cadence of Lockland's voice, which had been sterner than usual— "we don't trust Case until I say we do."

"Got it." I headed toward the door that would lead me to the street. "I wasn't planning on it." As I worked the locks, I murmured to myself, "That asshole hasn't earned it yet."

Chapter 2

Unlike the canals, which was fifteen to twenty meters underwater at its lowest point and covered in seekers, The North held its own risks. It was where able-bodied folks flouted government laws. Not put-up-your-dukes opposition, like Tandor had wanted—as in overthrow the government and burn what was left of the city to ashes—more thumbing their noses and waving their weapons in defiance of the rules they disliked.

Like, all of them.

It should've been called The Disgruntled North.

The inhabitants were always heavily armed and had a variety of watering holes called rathskells—skells, for short—where they congregated to trade goods and complain about their crappy lives. Skells catered to outskirts—individuals from out of town or those who'd been kicked out of the city for breaking the law.

I had a bunch of salvaging contacts in The North,

which was what led to my residence there. When you found a perfect location, one that was easily defensible, discreet, and vacant, it was hard to pass up. But The North was my least-favorite place to frequent in the city. Honestly, I'd take a rage-filled seeker over a pissed-off Northerner.

Seekers were predictable in their crazy, Northerners were not.

Other than The North and the canals, the city contained two more "official" areas. The Middle, where Bender lived, was one. It was guarded ferociously by its residents, who mainly wanted peace and quiet and to be left alone. And Government Square, which was made up of families and government workers, and contained the biggest span of uninterrupted blocks in the entire city, a kilometer square.

Government Square was where you found the Food Dispensary, where once a week we swiped the embedded tags on our wrists and received our protein cakes and the ever-delicious, thirst-quenching amino water, the cloudy brown drink of the bold and hardy. It was also where the Medi Center was located, where folks could go and wait for days to be treated, oftentimes dying first. And the Clothing Store, where you received a bland uniform if you didn't have the funds to hire a seamstress to sew together clothing you'd salvaged from other places.

There used to be other services as well, like an Energy Office to supply you with a few batteries so you could get by, and a Residence Assistance Office to help you locate a home that wasn't about to fall down around your head. But those offices had shut down or been whittled away to nothing over the last thirty years. Once The Water Initiative—where the elite had set out to sea with all our remaining resources—had taken place, the government had its hands full solving multiple crises, like finding enough slurry to fill the bio-printers so we all didn't starve to death and trying to save as many lives as possible at the Medi Center.

The mass exodus and loss of supplies had started a downward spiral. We were on track for mass extinction in less than ten years. It was best not to linger on it overmuch. It was too depressing.

After a kilometer and a half on foot, I finally reached the boundary line. Entry to The North at this particular point was marked by a five-meter-tall wall of debris and a handmade sign that blared:

> *We Don Fucking want U Heer.*
> *Enter at UR own Fucking Risk!*

It wasn't the words that would stop someone, because the intelligence behind the message was suspect at best. It was the fact that it'd been painted in blood, with a brush that very well could've been made from human hair, judging by the uneven, stringy strokes. Then there were the plethora of laser holes and scorch marks covering it from one side to the other, making the message harder to read.

It was meant to intimidate, and it had likely made a

few turn back and rethink their plans. But the sign didn't faze me. I immediately began to pick my way up and over the debris, moving at a quick clip. Coming in on foot was not my preferred method. Being without Luce sucked, especially since my residence was accessible only by craft, and once I arrived, I was going to have to get creative to figure out a way to ascend twelve stories without being seen.

I'd tackle that when I got there.

Just over the top, my foot slipped and I tumbled down a few meters before catching myself. Then, realizing it was easier, I slid the rest of the way down. "Well, that was fun," I muttered as I brushed myself off, kicking a piece of stubborn garbage off my foot as I began what would likely be an interesting trek through a temperamental neighborhood.

My first stop was a hidey-hole located in an uninhabited building a half kilometer from here. That should be easy enough. Shoving my gloved hands into my pockets as light drizzle bounced off my helmet and shoulders, I took off. My boots caused the occasional splash when they hit the inevitable minefield of rust-colored puddles, but other than that, there was nothing blocking my path.

As I walked, I tried not to worry about Daze.

I'd given him instructions to get back in the medi-pod for his daily treatment, knowing I'd be gone well into the night. The kid had multiple broken bones—one in his hand, another in his arm—and a cracked rib. He was also malnourished and dehydrated, which was common for inhabitants of this city. I figured Case would keep track of him, but I had no real idea if that would be the case or not. Thinking of Case being "on the case" cracked me up, and I giggled out loud.

"Somethin' funny there, missy?"

The voice, coming from the alcove of the building, surprised me, my hand instinctively going to my waist, my hips pivoting toward the threat.

I stopped just short of a full draw and squinted, my Gem already out of the holster, my fingers tight around the handle.

The figure in front of me was completely shrouded in fabric. But it wasn't your average sheeting—it was burial cloth.

The stuff we used to wrap dead bodies in before we lit them on fire. It was distinctive because of its metallic sheen and faint smell of accelerant. I leaned forward, sniffing the air. "Cozzi, is that you?" I asked. I'd recognized his voice, even though I couldn't see his face.

The figure seemed to catch himself, startled he'd been addressed directly. Then, very slowly, a pair of grizzled hands came up to tug the stuff back. I had to wait, not so patiently, as he struggled to uncover the mass bunched around his face. After some significant crinkling and swearing, he managed to free his head. He leaned toward me, coaxing his bloodshot eyes to focus with some rapid blinking.

It took a while.

"Holly?"

"Yep, it's me. I thought that was you. How are you, Cozzi? It's been a long time." His barely there snow-white hair was plastered to his head. If I was sweaty under my helmet, he looked as though he'd just gotten out of a cleaning stall without punching the dry cycle. "Why in the world are you standing in a dirty alcove wrapped in burial cloth? Please enlighten me."

His face broke into a wide grin. More teeth were missing than when I'd seen him last, particularly the front bunch. "Holly Danger, well, well, well." Then, surprisingly, he threw his arms out and came shuffling over. The cloth kept his movements to a minimum. "I can't believe it! I didn't think I'd have the pleasure of ever laying eyes on you again."

The physical aspect of our reunion was unexpected, but I allowed it, and even leaned in to facilitate a quick hug. Why not? I'd known Cozzi almost my entire life. It was a happy chance to find him here. I curled my nose as accelerant and the odor of unwashed body wafted up my nostrils, trying not to sputter as I stepped back. "Cozzi, why are you dressed in fire-probable clothing? One small spark and you're a goner. If you can't get down to the Clothing Store to get a new uniform, I can help you out. I have something that might fit at my residence."

He tottered backward a few steps, his sweaty head, missing teeth, and unusual outfit not detracting from his jovial disposition. "Oh, no! I prefer it this way. Keeps me warm and snug."

I quirked my head, spotting his belongings piled up

next to the wall. They were spilling out haphazardly. Cozzi had always been eccentric, but this was beyond his usual. His cherished residence was located just a few blocks from here. I'd taken cover there in my youth on more than a few occasions, the old man always making room for me and giving me his share of food and water. Nothing less than a massive threat could've gotten him out of his beloved home—it was as quirky as he was, littered with broken objects that no one knew the use for any longer.

"Why is all your stuff here? What the hell happened?" I shot him a bewildered look. "And don't even think about lying to me." There was no way I was going to accept his "warm and snug" answer or that he'd acquired a new fetish for wrapping himself in flammable clothing.

His face took on a fearful expression, his eyes darting away from mine. "I…um…decided to leave. The place was getting too cramped, you see…I needed some space…"

I crossed my arms, hip out, shoulder back, chin down, eyes hooded. It was my take-zero-shit pose. I'd perfected it over the years. Mimicking Bender as a young child had helped. "Nope. Try again."

"Well…I…needed a change of scenery, because…"

"No."

"My landlord…"

This time, I just shook my head.

He finally bowed his shiny, slippery head in defeat. "I can't tell you, Holly. Please trust an old man on this.

If I tell you, it'll bring you trouble. Big trouble. It's all better left unsaid."

I dropped my arms and the sass. His voice had been a mix of sadness and fear. I knew that pairing well. But it was Cozzi, and I had to help him. This man had been there for me in his own way for years and years. "You know that's not how I do things, Coz. I need to know what's up so I can help you—"

"*Please.*" His eyes would barely meet mine, his voice stressed to the breaking point. The next part came out in breathy stutters. "Don't…don't make me…tell you. At least not right now. Just…just…leave me and be on your way. Go, shoo, shoo." He actually flicked his wrist, like that, in and of itself, would make me take off.

I considered pushing the issue, but decided against it. I had no idea how many breaths Cozzi had left in him, and I didn't want to trigger a stroke or anything like that by forcing him to do something he didn't want to do. "Fine. You don't have to tell me right now. But I'm getting you out of here." I brushed by him to pick up his belongings. "Unwrap yourself from that cloth, so we can get going." I hefted up the two heaviest bags, one of which was a duffel that I slung over my shoulder, and stepped onto the sidewalk. The other two bags were smaller. He could manage those.

Cozzi stared at me, unmoving, like he'd never been more confused. "But…but I can't go with you."

"Why not? How many times in the past have you opened your door to me? I'm pretty sure you saved my life on a few occasions." I couldn't take him to my residence. That would be too risky. But I had a feasible option. Ignoring Cozzi's mystified expression as the tip of his pink tongue poked in and out of the empty holes, I dragged a small tech phone out of my vest pocket and depressed a button, bringing it to my lips. "Jerry, it's Ella." I paused, giving Lockland time to react. "Is seventeen free? I need to use it tonight for a friend." We always spoke in code, as anyone with an amplifier could listen in.

Static came over the line first, then, "It's free. Don't know how the last guests left it, so you might have to clean it up and bring your own linen." Lockland was telling me that he had no idea if seventeen, our safe house in The North, had been compromised, so be careful.

"Will do."

Darby knew the locations of all of our safe houses. There was no way to know whether Tandor and his crew had uncovered the location of seventeen with their Babble injection, or how many of Tandor's men had survived the confrontation last night. We were going to have to be more alert than usual for a while.

"That's a mighty fine unit," Cozzi said, nodding at my phone as I tucked it back into my vest. "I had one once. Hard to come by these days."

Longwave radio was the only way to communicate in a world filled with iron dust. High frequency couldn't get through, so it was a good thing there had been other options. It was too bad the meteor hadn't been made of something less intrusive to everyday living. But there was no way to undo it. And it'd been done in spectacular fashion.

"Let's go, Cozzi," I instructed. "I'm taking you to a safe place temporarily, until I can figure out what's going on. There's enough food and water for about a week or two. But in order to get there, you're going to have to unwind yourself from that burial sheet." I gestured with my shoulder toward his ridiculous outfit. "And can you hurry it up?" Seventeen wasn't that far off my route and, conveniently, was on the way to my cache. When Cozzi turned a particular shade of red, brightened by the silver sheen of the fabric cowled around his neck, my eyebrows rose. "Please tell me you have clothing on underneath that sheet."

"Well...I..."

"Cozzi, seriously, what the *hell*?" When the old man looked like he might cry, I backed off. "Forget it." I dumped the duffel on the ground and reached into a pocket for my cutter. "Ever heard of a toga?"

Chapter 3

Hustling Cozzi through the streets, laden with all his worldly possessions, wasn't the easiest task in the world, but I'd done harder. By the time we came to a stop in front of the correct building, the old man was wheezing and huffing—and he was carrying the small stuff. I had no idea how he'd managed to lug all his belongings as far as he had to begin with, and I didn't ask. No use stressing him out further. I had my eye on the prize—getting him to safety so I could continue my day.

He glanced upward, shielding his eyes. Along with an expletive, he brought his gaze around to mine, his mouth dangling open, exposing the many hollow spaces lurking inside. "We can't go in there." His tone was resolute. When I looked nonplussed, he frantically gestured to the painted symbols on the walls, most of them indicating that harm would come to anyone who trespassed. Something that worked like a charm in The

North, but was totally ignored in the canals. Seekers, to a one, didn't stop to contemplate anything written on the wall, no matter how decorative or deadly it was. "That's…that's…charted territory," he sputtered.

The universal expression in The North for *somebody else's claim.*

"We're going in," I said, my tone final. I refrained from telling him it was ours. Nobody was on the street, but that didn't mean people weren't listening. People were always listening. When he didn't make a move to enter, I nudged his backside. "Stop acting like a baby nibbling on his first protein cake and get your ass inside. These bags are heavy. Did you pack your steel-rod collection?" When Cozzi refused to move, I butted in front of him, stepping through the opening, crunching over the crap scattered on the floor.

I headed directly toward a specific wall which would lead us to the internal stairway, ten meters to the left, setting down the bags once I arrived. Clanking ensued. Not steel rods, but something equally as heavy. Probably his collection of cups and plates. He was known to hoard.

Reluctant footsteps shuffled behind me. "I don't know about this——"

"How about you let me worry about the logistics?" I shot a wry glance over my shoulder. "I've managed to get you mostly out of your flammable shroud and into a safe place in less than fifteen minutes. Now would be a good time to stop arguing with me and start lavishing praise." While he pondered my request, I peeled off a glove, lifted my hand to a section of the wall that ran parallel to the stairwell, and rested my open palm on the upper right quadrant. I had to wait only a few seconds before a click sounded, and the wall, which was actually a painted panel of graphene, popped open.

Behind me, there was a gasp, followed by a ragged cough.

When the hacking didn't readily ease up, I turned and pounded a fist on Cozzi's back. "Come on, Coz, you shouldn't be this overcome. You know I have resources. I haven't seen you in a while, but this shouldn't shock you into a heart attack in your burial gear, although you'd clearly be ready." He looked totally crazy. Where were his clothes anyway? Did he get pushed out of his place so fast he didn't even have time to get dressed? He was one of the oldest inhabitants in the city. He had to be at least sixty or seventy. Living that long around here was an accomplishment—an *accomplishment*. He was also a fan favorite, even in The Disgruntled North.

I eyed him as his coughing fit subsided between gasps and new starts. "I'm not overcome, I'm impressed." His words were injected with some of the old pizzazz I remembered. It was good to hear. "I'm just a little bit miffed it took you so long to show me."

Tossing my head back, I chortled, happy I was in a position to help him after all these years. Cozzi grinned. Standing this close, I realized that his eyes weren't merely bloodshot, like I'd first thought. It looked like some blood vessels were ruptured. Whatever had happened to him, it hadn't been pretty.

"I mean...I knew you were grown and self-sufficient," he said, "but I had no idea those symbols were linked to you. They're all over this damn city!"

"They are indeed." I nodded. "The only reason you didn't know before is because we haven't seen each other in too many years. You know I hate coming to The North. People here are pissy as hell. That, and it's taken me more than a few years to learn to share. It's a relatively new skill, so don't push it. Come on." I picked up the bags, ignoring the rattling as I shouldered them. "Follow my lead exactly, or you'll have an immediate use for that burial shroud. The symbols don't lie." I stepped through the opening in the wall.

"You'll have to find me a new cloth if I die. You've ruined this one. Now only my midsection will burn."

I snorted. "You're not perishing on my watch. You've got about a hundred stubborn years left in you, old man. Just make sure you step over that"—I nodded toward the trip wire on the floor—"and we're good."

Thankfully, it didn't take me long to get Cozzi settled. The safe house was a single room in the basement. I had no idea if anyone else inhabited the building above, and I wasn't planning to find out.

I'd instructed Cozzi to stay put and that I'd check on him when I had a chance. I hoped it would be within a week, but I didn't promise him anything. He seemed content to wait it out, not offering up any further details about why I'd found him wrapped like a wick with all his belongings scattered behind him.

I'd get it out of him eventually.

My head was bowed as I continued down a side street. It was still relatively early, and thankfully, The North was known for taking the mornings off. Blackout was prime time around here. By my count, I had roughly six hours to get my stuff done and get back to Bender's. Even with the Cozzi interruption, I should have plenty of time.

Two blocks down, I took a right, then zigzagged across the street, making my way around a few piles of refuse, including several gigantic hunks of steel and a load of cables, which had been used to provide the city with power once upon a time.

Directly after the meteor struck, there hadn't been any resources to do a full cleanup, and over time, the trash and debris had been relocated to giant heaps, so people could move through the streets. This was as good as it got. Nobody bothered anymore, as there was more where that came from. Pieces of buildings and debris fell from abandoned scrapers on a regular basis.

I took a left and ducked into a nondescript building, one that'd been sheared off three stories up. This building had no painted symbols to warn anyone away, because no one would come here anyway, for fear it would crumble down around them. It was literally on the verge of collapse.

My cache was on the second floor.

Stepping in the spots I'd reinforced, I ascended the rickety interior staircase, listening as I went. I'd stored several important items here in recent months—a coveted gypsy motor not too long ago and an oversized cooling unit, one that barely fit in Luce's passenger seat. I'd had to fly with the door up, landing on the street outside at dawn. Then I'd strapped the thing to my back to get it up the stairs.

I'd already had a buyer, so it'd been worth it.

But I hadn't come here for either of those items.

The prize I needed I'd stored over three years ago. Problem was, I couldn't exactly remember where I'd put the damn thing. It was incredibly lethal, so I'd made a point of storing it someplace special. One I just couldn't recall. My memory wasn't failing at twenty-seven, but with all the stuff that had been going on in my head these last few days, I guess I shouldn't be too surprised. It must be my brain's way of telling me that I needed a vacation.

The notion made me laugh out loud.

At the top of the second landing, I eased into the hallway. It was clear, no sounds erupting anywhere, except for the crunching under my feet and the inevitable creak and groan as the building listed in the breeze. If it came down eventually, I would ultimately lose some things, but it wouldn't be the end of the world. The protection this location afforded me by having no one snooping around was priceless.

Flipping my helmet visor up, I grabbed my chromoscope glasses out of my front pocket and slid them on, flicking the dial to ultraviolet. I'd sprinkled powder all over the first floor and the steps. If anyone had been up here, the tracks would be vivid.

No footprints.

I made my way toward the room, my back against the wall, my ass sliding along the surface in an effort to keep a low profile. Once I was situated across from my door, I tucked the glasses back into my vest and pulled out my audio amplifier, which was no bigger than a pebble, and inserted it into my ear. I'd tossed my last one away fighting Tandor, and was lucky I had a few spares. It slid in smoothly, fitting snugly in my canal. I stepped forward and rested my head against the wall to the right of the opening.

No noise came from inside.

The audio amplifier would pick up even the faintest sounds, since I had a mic set up inside. If someone was sleeping in there, I'd be able hear the even tones of their breathing. This particular room was internal to the building, no windows to the outside.

I was almost in. One last thing.

As I picked the amplifier out of my ear, I patted my vest. It took me a few tries to remember in which pocket I'd stored my door poppers. I finally found them, pulling out six extremely thin steel tubes hooked on a ring, each with its own welded nugget in a specific shape on the bottom. One of the six matched this particular door lock. If I didn't choose the right one, it would set off a chain reaction that would explode a hydro-bomb big enough to raze this precarious building.

I grumbled as I picked my way through the steel tubes, searching for the right one. I didn't have them marked, but if I chose wrong, it would be a very bad day. I hit one of my shoulder lights, and hazy blue light lit a one-meter space around me. The six openers were fanned out in my palm. I finally plucked out the one with the nugget shaped like an F.

I'd fashioned an F for this location because it fucking sucked. How could I forget that?

I stuck the key in the slot and turned. A click sounded, and the door sprang open. I squeezed through the small opening. The door wouldn't give any farther than a meter, because there was so much junk piled behind it—junk, meaning stacks of valuable, prized possessions.

Closing it behind me, I pocketed the tube with the crusty F on it and hit the button on the wall. Enough yellow light erupted so I could see. My lights were battery-powered, rigged up simply. Everything stored here was densely packed, leaving only a narrow path. I glanced around and, as always, was amazed at how much I'd amassed and what I was still able to find sixty years after disaster had struck.

Placing my hands on my hips, I bit my lip. Now, where did I put that thing?

Moving forward, I knelt next to a box of random fasteners and slid them out of the way. A jangle sounded, and as they clinked together, the noise sparked my memory. I moved another box, this one containing carbon cups. Something Cozzi might like. I had to locate a space on the wall, so I crawled ahead, shifting things as I went.

Finally where I needed to be, I peeled off a glove and slid my bare hand along the cool surface until I came in contact with what I was looking for. Pinching the tiny tab, which was made out of clear rubber, I popped the panel off. It released with a small suction noise and plopped into my open hand. I set it aside and reached for the goods.

With the utmost care, I pulled out my treasure.

It was wrapped in a thin cloth made of steel fiber.

Unfolding the protective covering, I looked at the object sitting there, a tiny stone in the middle of my palm. It was incredible that something so small could harness such deadly power. But when you were talking about radioactive compounds, size didn't really matter.

It was all about the energy transfer, and once activated, it would mess you up.

Chapter 4

Once I had my scary, lethal prize, I locked up and skedaddled. No reason to stick around. I'd wrapped the radium ball back up in its containment cloth and carefully placed it inside a small pocket in my vest. I'd have to twist it to activate it, but it still made me nervous carrying it around. The double-steel core inside was pressurized—from what I'd uncovered about them, since I'd never used one before—and when detonated, the insides heated up and radiation seeped out, infecting anything in its path.

It would be a fatal dose.

Radium balls had been a secret weapon created by the government for use during covert wars long before the dark days.

I'd found this one by chance at a residence that used to house a government spy. Well, at least I thought he was a spy. Nothing labeled him as such, but based on the contents I'd found inside the safe I'd cracked—like, literally cracked with a sledge and a well-positioned hydro-bomb—it seemed like he was. There'd been various forms of paper identification—none that had been used in the last hundred years—all with the same picture but different names. It'd been kind of fun imagining what this guy used to do. The radium ball had been kept in a steel box, along with some other out-of-date tech.

I'd been damn lucky I hadn't inadvertently activated it during the safe-cracking. By my best guess, the last and final occupant of the residence hadn't known the safe existed. It'd been deeply set into a wall, and the guy whose picture was on the ID's had been long dead.

But, like everything else around here, there was no way of ever knowing.

Outside, there was movement on the street. People were waking up. I kept my head down, hands jammed in my pockets, trying to achieve an unassuming posture. I wasn't looking for any trouble, even though I had no doubt it would find me at some point.

My residence was at least ten blocks away, and when I arrived, I'd have to figure out how to get myself up to the twelfth story of a building that was inhabited by people on the lower floors—and was virtually impassable from floors eight to twelve.

Damn, I wished I had Luce. Life sucked without a craft.

I was four blocks from my building when an angry shout assaulted my ears.

It'd been directed at me.

"Who are you?" the voice raged. "And what are you doing on *my* fucking street?"

I put my game face on. An altercation was inevitable, but that didn't mean I had to like it. I kept walking, not giving my antagonist the pleasure of my attention. "Just passing through," I replied loudly enough to be heard.

"Stop right there, or I'll blow your goddamn brains all over the sidewalk."

I stopped.

"That's a pretty sweet vest you've got there. Haven't seen one of those before."

That's because I had it custom made, asshole.

The voice had come from across the street. Not only one man, there were two sets of footsteps. He wasn't alone.

Fingering my Gem, I waited patiently for his approach without turning. After giving him a moment to get within my proximity, I said, "I'd cease coming any closer if you value a beating heart. I want no trouble. I'm just making my way through." I'd uttered the words in my most *don't fuck with me* tone. That usually did the trick—or at least made someone ponder the implications of my threat.

Not this guy. He made a sound resembling a snort mixed with a huff, asserting himself. He could tell I was female. Not only did my hair, which was long and hung out the back of my helmet, give it away, but so did my curves. I wore formfitting synthetic leather from head to toe. It was warm and offered me the best unimpeded movement in this dark, dank, dreary city.

"You think you scare me, you bit—"

I pivoted, crashing my elbow into his jaw.

He went down. Hard.

If I decided to kill him, and he was someone prominent in this community, it would be a hell of a mess, with all kinds of retribution. Not that I wouldn't do it to protect myself, because I would. Best to wait and see, and he wasn't a threat any longer as he was having trouble drawing a single breath into his lungs, his chest currently being crushed to the point of asphyxiation under my boot.

I stuck my Gem in his face. It was twice as big as the relic shooter he had curled in his fist, which I had pinched under my other toe. "Say it again," I snarled. "I dare you."

A line of blood trickled out of the side of his mouth, though he looked far from acquiescing. Such a shame. "You think you're tough? I'll show you—"

I bent over and coldcocked him with my free hand, ramming my fist into his temple, instead of his nose, as I still wasn't eager to kill him. He looked like a street punk, not a mastermind of criminal activity. Knocking him out would suffice.

His head lolled to the side, and I stepped back, the print of my wet boot standing out on his bland canvas jacket. I turned, my Gem up, to see who was next.

Surprisingly, the guy in front of me appeared stunned, his hands already rising from his sides in a surrender pose. "I don't want no trouble," he stammered, his voice shaky, his hands now all the way up. "I…I know who you are."

I kept my barrel locked on him. "Is that so?" My tone was bored. "You might've done your buddy a solid and warned him. Then we could've avoided this unpleasantness."

The guy's expression became slightly horrified, his thin lips dropping into a frown. He nodded at the guy, out cold, blood still dripping from his mouth onto the wet ground. "That's Dill. He's no friend of mine."

"Dill, huh?" I glanced down at the son of a bitch who thought he was a tough guy, like most Northerners. "More like Dill*weed*." I spat on the ground next to him, allowing my contempt to show.

The man looked confused. "What?"

"It's a plant. One that used to grow. People used it as a spice…never mind," I mumbled.

"A spice?" The guy wore no helmet. His stringy brown hair was streaked with gray and hung limply to his shoulders. He was tall and thin, his cheeks hollowed and covered with days' old growth. He looked nothing like Dill, who obviously ate his share of protein cakes and had to have coin, since his clothing was custom, judging by his duds.

"I said never mind." I holstered my Gem, wanting to get out of here before we attracted a crowd. "What's your name?"

"Is it true you took out that outskirt the other day? Blasted a hole right through him?" the guy asked, not bothering to answer my question.

I raised a single eyebrow.

Sharing information with strangers didn't happen. "I'm out of here. You might want to drag your friend inside. It would be a shame for him to get crushed by falling debris at this point, since I let him live and all." I turned to leave. There was immediate shuffling behind me. I took a few more steps, just to be sure, then spun around, this time drawing my taser. It was set to stun. A burst to his chest would hurt like hell. The electrical charge pulsed through the nervous system, clenching muscles painfully, ensuring that any victim stayed down for a good half hour.

If it was set to kill, this thing could stop a heart.

"Listen, asshole. It's not a good idea to follow me. Just turn around and scuttle back to where you came from and take the Dillweed with you." I flicked my wrist, causing the taser to bob in the international sign of *get lost and do it quickly before I change my mind.*

The guy still had his hands raised, but instead of taking my advice, he skittered a step closer, stammering, "I…I can get you information."

My eyebrows quirked again, but this time slightly less satirically. I was confused. In this city, one didn't ignore an offer of information. The more you had, the more you lived. "What's it going to cost me?"

"Protection…I want protection." As I watched, his face began to convey some Cozzi-like expressions. Worry, uncertainty, and a low-level fear flitted across his gaunt features.

A Northerner was asking me for protection.

What the *hell* was going on?

This day wasn't supposed to be unusual, dammit. Life was supposed to go back to something more predictable, even though I had a kid and stuff. "Why do you need protection?" I asked, my taser still up. This guy could be playing me, which I detested. I'd been fooled enough in the past few days to last ten lifetimes.

Real fear showed in his eyes, along with a dose of uncertainty. He rolled his bottom lip. It caught under one grimy, protruding tooth, which scraped along his stubble, making a scratching sound as he debated what he could share. "I can't say just yet."

I turned to leave. I didn't have time to dicker with noninformation.

"Wait!" he called to my retreating back.

"Sorry, guy," I tossed over my shoulder. "I don't work in half deals. I have places to be." Footsteps began to shuffle after me, quicker this time. I wasn't going to lose this guy unless I tased him, which was sounding more and more appealing. I turned, less gracefully this time, annoyed that he was still tagging after me, and walked backward as I talked. "Listen, I told you, I don't work in I'll-trade-you-now-for-info-later. If you have something to share in return for protection, you have to lay it out for me and make the deal worthwhile. Otherwise, stop wasting my time. Isn't there a skell you can pop into to hobnob with your fellow Northerners about this? I'm pretty sure plenty of them would jump at a job if the price was right. Northerners live for that shit." I nodded toward the guy's waistband, which was devoid of anything to defend himself. "And just a suggestion, the first thing you may want to do is invest in a weapon of some kind. Even a half-tase is better than nothing."

It seemed I'd spoken too many words for this guy to process at once. His tooth sprang out from between his lips again, and I almost tased him right there so I wouldn't have to listen to the scratching. Must be a nervous tic. "Northerners aren't enough for what's coming," he finally managed.

I stopped. Since when were Northerners not enough? "Nobody loves a fight more than a North—"

A clattering noise came from between two buildings across the street. My attention shot toward it, my taser following. Dill was still out cold thirty paces away.

Less than three seconds later, a body stumbled into sight. It was a female. Her movements were irregular, her limbs jerking, her feet shuffling like her legs had forgotten how to work.

I knew that gait anywhere.

My gaze shifted, landing firmly on the guy in front of me. "What's a seeker doing in The North? You've got half a second to answer before I shoot you." My free hand unholstered my Gem.

The guy's hands were still in the air, although lower, his eyes pinned on the seeker who was continuing to stumble our way. "The men have Plush. I'm not supposed to say—"

Dill groaned loudly as he stuck his head up, followed by a shrill, "What the fuck just happened?"

He sat up, rubbing the side of his head, a pissed-off expression on his face, clear from this distance. He was going to have a hell of a bruise. Sometimes my work was extremely satisfying.

As we watched, the seeker changed direction slightly, stumbling toward the asshole on the ground. He'd be an easier target for her next fix.

Breathy moans shot from her mouth, along with garbled words like *need* and *pleasure.*

I knocked the guy in front of me on the shoulder with the barrel of my Gem, getting his attention, which had been utterly diverted by the seeker. Without knowing it, he'd scooted closer, like I was a rod of steel and he was a magnet. "As you were saying?"

Startled, he whipped his head toward me.

I'd scared him, which hadn't been at all hard to do. The guy seemed like he lived in a perpetual state of unease. I was surprised he actually had any stubble ringing his bottom lip. It should've been scraped off a long time ago. He was about to say something when Dill jumped to his feet, swaying a little, his hand going up to brace his head, spouting, "Ned, get away from that bitch. We have things to do!" He ignored the seeker, who was three meters from him and closing.

This was a huge red flag.

About as red as it gets.

People in The North didn't have to deal with seekers, because they kept their neighborhoods protected. And even if a seeker did show up, they wouldn't last more than an hour or two at most, since most Northerners would love the chance for a little target practice.

Not to mention, Dill was not in the least alarmed.

In fact, as we watched, he withdrew something from his waist. "Mary"—his voice projected irritation—"I thought I told you to stay inside. This is not your battle."

Mary?

I was about to convey my thoughts on how fucked up the matter was when Ned turned, his eyeballs doing a crazy dance as he mouthed, *Get out of here.*

The message could not have been conveyed any clearer, especially since we were standing close enough for his rank breath to steal up my nose. I nodded once.

As I backed away, I watched over Ned's shoulder as Dill set a hand on the seeker's shoulder and stuck a dart straight into her forehead.

She collapsed into his arms, and he began to drag her away.

What. The. Hell.

Chapter 5

I couldn't get the image of Dill and Mary out of my head as I made my way down the streets, this time at a much quicker pace. I wasn't going to be stopped a second time, and if anyone tried, they were not going to survive the event. That had been some of the craziest shit I'd seen in a long time.

Nothing added up.

Not Cozzi, not Ned, not the Dillweed, and certainly not the seeker.

Trying to make sense of it all, I ducked into an alcove made of bent steel girders and old stone blocks right across from the entrance to my building. "This city has lost its mind," I mumbled, angling my head up to spot the twelfth story. My home. Drizzle pelted my visor, rolling off without impeding my view, but it was still hard to see, as the clouds were dark, obscuring anything above the fifth floor. "How the hell am I going to get up there?"

A noise came from my left.

Footsteps.

If whoever was passing decided to investigate this spot, there could be trouble. I tucked myself into the nook as far as I could go, my black outfit benefiting me in these situations.

I noticed the height of the man first, followed by the sweeping trench.

The figure passed without glancing my way, head down. "What the hell are you doing here, Case?" I called to his retreating form, my voice irritated. "I thought you went to be with the kid after you dropped me off this morning."

Case stopped and backed up. The part of his face I could see beneath his visor showed no expression whatsoever. For a split second, it made me miss Ned, whose expression had been freakishly exposed and readily interpreted.

Then I remembered his wandering tooth.

"In the future, you might want to be a little more guarded," I said, "and remember to check all the nooks and crannies as you pass by, especially in this neighborhood."

"I have business here," he said by way of answering, which really wasn't an answer. Typical. "The kid will be fine." He was right, and I was showing all the signs of a fretting mother. What was wrong with me? Daze was back at the barracks, basically holed up in the lap of luxury—as lux as it got around here—with enough food and water and shelter to keep him nourished and safe for weeks on end. A big change from his former life. Just as long as he didn't try to escape, which I'd drilled into his head a hundred times before I left. If he tried to get out, he'd blow himself up, or worse.

Yes, there was worse. He could blow off an arm and then just wish he was dead.

Case glanced around, seeming to recognize our surroundings for the first time. "What are you doing here?"

"None of your business."

He shrugged. He was just about to take off when I asked, "Is Seven close?" Case flew a matte black Q7. It handled like a dream, the fastest craft I'd ever handled.

His expression changed a teensy bit, but because I still didn't have a good view of his eyes under the visor, which was highly reflective, I could only partially guess what he was thinking. Best hypothesis was that he thought I'd lost some of my marbles. "Close enough."

How to ask this without sounding ridiculous? "Can I borrow her for about twenty minutes?" Shouldn't take me longer than that to stock up on some stuff and look for the reflective cloth Lockland needed.

He crossed his arms, not willing to give me the quick answer I'd been hoping for. I reached out and pulled him into the covered space with me. He came willingly, thankfully. We didn't need any witnesses noticing him loitering in the street.

Case was taller than I was, which was irritating, and he was all brawn. The man was militia, whether he was active now or not, which meant he'd been trained to fight. After the dark days, the military had evolved quickly, becoming an active militia, first as a protectorate, then as aggressive backers of the government.

Nowadays, because the militia was spread so thin, soldiers were mainly used as guards—as in, they protected the government from the angry townspeople who always wanted more. Honestly, could you blame us?

"So? Can I borrow her?" I tried to make my tone less bitchy and more amiable, since I needed something from this guy, but it pretty much sounded the same as always.

"Yeah," he said. "But I go with."

I shook my head. "Nope. That's not how this is going to go."

"It's how it goes, or you don't get it."

"*Her.* Seven is a her. I can't believe I'm trying to negotiate with a guy who never bothered to name his craft." I was superstitious like that. I positioned a gloved hand on my hip and contemplated my options. I could leave and forget it, finding my own complicated way to the top of a building that had four torn-up stories between my residence and the last usable public floor. Or I could agree to his stupid terms. Or I could barter. I chose the latter. "Fine. You go, but you stay in the craft."

He shook his head.

The space in the alcove was tight, and I was getting

antsy. I leaned forward, my expression hard. "Fine. You come in, I lead you over a trip wire, you blow yourself up, and I get my stuff *and* inherit a great craft for my sweet, barely strained efforts."

"My craft is trapped. You won't get very far." He was irritatingly unaffected by my awesome murder option.

"Come on, Case." My tone was impatient. "I need my stuff, and you have a craft that you're currently not using. Twenty minutes, tops. I'll have her back and parked at your desired location before you're done with whatever business you have here." What business *did* he have here?

"Either I go, or no deal."

I huffed, angling my head out to gaze up at floor twelve. Only, I couldn't see it because it was dark and cloudy and the rain was coming down harder now. Getting up there on my own would be a bitch, not to mention it could take me all day.

Note to self: Make a cable swing for future use.

Time to level with Case and up the ante. I dropped my hand and assumed a casual stance. My body felt odd, because all I wanted to do was throat-punch him and take his craft. I was trying for civil. That should count for something. "Listen, a bunch of strange shit just happened. I encountered a seeker here, and there hasn't been a seeker in this neighborhood since before I was born. Not only that, but this guy, Dill, controlled her with a dart to the forehead. He wasn't scared at all. He called her Mary. I don't know about you, but that was unsettling, especially after everything that just happened with Tandor. I need to get my supplies and get back to my crew so we can find our other friend, who's in government holding, so we can get to the bottom of this." I wasn't going to tell him about Cozzi or what Ned had said. He didn't need *all* the details, just the basic gloss, conveyed in a semibegging tone with my body nice and relaxed. See? I could play nice.

"I know."

My expression shot to perplexed, followed by stark irritation. "You know *what?*"

"There's been talk."

Case could be as nonverbal as Darby when he wanted to be. "Talk about what, exactly? Quit with the runaround. Be specific."

One of his lips attempted a quirk, but it was gone just as quickly. He was enjoying stringing me along. "I'll tell you more when we get to where we're going." His arms were still firmly locked in front of his broad chest, and they weren't going anywhere.

Fuck.

"You're like a needle inserted directly into the eye, Case. Fine. We go, but if you get blown up, it's not my fault. And I *will* take Seven after your untimely death. Your traps don't scare me." They kind of did, but he didn't need to know that. I was pretty sure if I tripped on one of his wires, I wasn't going to get tasespray in the eye. I'd probably end up with a fist-sized laser hole running through my temple. "Where is she parked?"

Without another word, he turned, heading back the way he'd come. I swore under my breath. I had no choice but to follow along like a lackey, vibrating with vengeful irritation the entire way.

Thankfully, we didn't encounter anyone over the next few blocks. I was curious to see where Case had parked. The only times I'd ever taken Luce into this neighborhood, before I'd set up my residence, I'd parked outside and walked in. I wasn't willing to risk any damage to my craft.

Surprisingly, Case headed into a building I knew housed residents. He walked into the main staircase like he owned the place. I was tempted to grab him by the elbow and demand an explanation, but that would've taken too much time, and I was beyond curious at this point.

This building wasn't very tall, and as we rounded the sixth story, we came to the top, an exposed roof that had been sheared off fairly cleanly. Seven was sitting a few meters away, not a scratch on her. "How in the hell—"

I was cut off by a sound to my left as a man emerged from what looked to be a lean-to in the corner. He was old, but not Cozzi old. Maybe fifty. He was also incredibly mean-looking, with haggard features, overly bushy eyebrows that had jets of hair shooting every which way, and perhaps a glass eye, since it didn't move or blink as he addressed us.

"Pay up!" His voice came out as a high-pitched squeak with some spittle at the end. He held out a gloved hand that was missing at least three fingertips, the rest on the verge of unraveling.

I watched as Case dipped into the pocket of his trench and brought out a few coins. The man greedily shoved the funds into drooping pants, then turned and shuffled back into the lean-to.

Like nothing had just happened, Case made his way to Seven, lifting the pilot's-side door to get in.

"Oh, no, you don't," I demanded before he could fold his body inside. "I'm flying." He gave me a look, but it was my turn to shake my head. Without further argument, he made his way around to the passenger side, and I took the helm. The way the world intended. I closed the door and gave him a look. It carried some wonder. "How did you know you could pay for parking here? I thought you were from down South." I narrowed my gaze. "And an outskirt like you shouldn't be as comfortable as you are in The North. They like outskirts here, to be sure, but they're always leery of outsiders. That old man didn't even blink at you. And maybe he couldn't, because of his crazy glass eye, but still. He acted like you were best friends."

Case's expression didn't even pretend to shift. "All he wanted was his coin. And I'm a quick learner."

"Bullshit," I muttered as I punched the craft on, giving Case a huge side-eye that he probably didn't see because he was looking out his window. "And I better not get any tasespray in the face after I take off." Seven's controls felt comfortable in my grasp. The levers were slightly larger than Luce's and moved with zero resistance. It made flying tricky if you didn't have any finesse.

I engaged the propulsion, and we rose off the roof.

"Tasespray is for rookies," Case replied. Before I could comment, he added, "And don't even think about it. I'm not wearing a blindfold."

I swore under my breath. Sparring with Case was a full-time job—one I didn't have energy for at the moment. "You can at least give me the courtesy of closing your eyes." Not that that would help, as he would likely recognize the building since we'd been standing in front of it five minutes ago. This meant I would have to come back and set new traps, which would be exhausting.

Instead of closing his eyes, he turned to me, his voice matter-of-fact. "Up ahead, turn right, three buildings down, land in the hidey-hole on the twelfth floor."

I gritted my teeth.

Case knew where my residence was.

Exactly where it was.

I accelerated Seven up into the air at full throttle, causing the know-it-all to launch backward in his seat, bang his head, and shout an expletive. "How do you like that?" I muttered. "You're not winning this round, you bastard. I am."

Chapter 6

I landed Seven smoothly on her rubber landing pads in a space less than two meters bigger than she was. Turning her off, I sat back in my seat. "I wasn't kidding before about blowing yourself up," I told my unwelcome passenger. "If you don't follow my movements until we get inside, you will perish. I promise, though, I'll only take the adequate amount of pleasure in your demise, nothing more."

"Good to know."

We opened our doors and squeezed out. It was easier for me to maneuver around in the small space than the guy who was almost a half a meter taller and had double the body mass. The craft sat inside what used to be an apartment unit that had since been obliterated. My residence was next door. I skirted a few piles of debris, partially hoping Case didn't catch up. It would be nice if he tumbled off the building and I could finally be done. I wasn't used to having a shadow, and everything about it bugged me. Other than interacting with my crew a few times a month, I worked alone. Daze was going to be an adjustment, but I was resigned to that fact. After all, I'd offered that deal up to him without a laser pressed to my temple. The fact that I had was still confusing.

But having an adult trailing after me was irritating.

At the back wall, farthest from the opening where the rain poured in thin sheets, I tugged a laser key out of my pocket. It was the size of my thumb, and I palmed it, hoping Case didn't see what I was using. I depressed the button, aiming it into the hole. This laser was a particular frequency and color, amethyst. There weren't a ton of laser keys around, but it was a good way to lock stuff up if you could find one. The door popped. I scowled rather than smiled, thinking again of how Case's presence meant I'd have to reinforce this place later.

I scooted through the gap, not leaving it open for him. If the door closed, Case would have to wait outside. Not my fault. If he didn't move around the area, he'd survive.

His arm managed to sneak in and brace it before it fully shut. He followed me, grunting in the process. The door was heavy. The short hallway ended in what appeared to be a solid wall made of graphene. I snapped on a shoulder light while ordering, "Turn around and face the other way." I dug around in my pockets, making a lot of extra noise so Case had no idea what I was grabbing. I withdrew the steel tubes

I'd just used at my last place while Case kept his back to me. I tapped one of the tubes against the door to make a clicking sound that camouflaged my other, more stealthlike movements as my hand slid onto the quadrant that held the heat sensor, just like the one I'd used at seventeen to get Cozzi inside.

The beauty of a heat sensor was that almost no one had access to them. I'd been lucky enough to salvage a bunch when I was in my early teens, and I'd put them to good use over the years, with a little—okay, a fairly hefty amount of—help from Bender to get them operational. It was older technology that had been replaced by voice and retinal activation long ago. All our ancestors had had to do to operate almost anything was give it a command or place an eye to a sensor. VoiceRec had been highly accurate, based on a complicated system that monitored your timbre, cadence, tone, and a number of other things that were uniquely your own.

It was a convenience everyone had taken for granted. Must've been nice.

The wall in front of me gave a groan as it creaked open no more than five centimeters.

This was where things got trickier.

The door was tethered from the inside, and if I didn't unhook it just right, there would be an explosion. Not big enough to kill an intruder, but enough to make somebody think twice before entering.

Poking my arm through the slit, I felt around the shallow doorjamb. My hand curled around a meter-long stick with a small catch on the end. I angled it up toward a rubber binder attached to the hinge, carefully extracting it, my head jammed into the opening as far as the space would allow me to go.

Once the binder popped, the door swung wide and I walked into my residence. Case followed. The place had a musty smell, as most shut-up spaces did in our wet climate. I stepped to the side, allowing Case to get in front of me.

As soon as I closed the door behind us, I reached for my Gem, tugging it out of my waistband as I simultaneously hit a button on the wall.

The door to my wardrobe sprang open, smashing Case in the face as my foot snaked around his ankle. I brought him down effortlessly. He landed on his stomach with a grunt.

The wardrobe was a small distraction, but it was all I needed.

He rolled over, rubbing his face as my boot stomped on his abdomen. I had both hands around my Gem as I aimed it downward. He was about to respond, his face angry, when I cut him off. "How did you know where to find me on the street back there?" I wasn't playing anymore. "Don't fuck with me, Case. I want answers, and you're either going to give them, or you're going to die."

I'd played along with his crap, using him for the ride up. If he thought for even a second I'd fallen for his explanation that he'd stumbled onto me by accident, he was dumber than I thought. Then, when he confirmed the location of my residence, I'd been certain. It was a good thing I was a gifted actress, but acting was a talent that was rarely needed in this town.

I wanted answers, and he was going to give them to me.

By the surprised expression that had quickly replaced the anger, it was clear he hadn't been expecting this particular turn of events. Good. "I wasn't following you." He closed his eyes.

"Yeah, right. People don't just run into each other in this city. There's always a catch, a rhyme and a reason, a plan of some kind. How'd you find me? Did you inject me with a tracker again?" If he had, it would be the last thing he ever did.

"No."

"Not good enough, Case. I'm getting antsy." My voice conveyed my agitation. With one hand steady on my Gem, I withdrew the taser from my waist. If he didn't comply, I would use it, and then get hold of Lockland and Bender and see what they wanted to do.

Case sensed my seriousness, judging by the tension in his body, which was smart of him. My finger was itchy. "I figured you'd come north eventually, so I waited."

"And how did you figure such a thing?" I hadn't made any mention of my plans this morning when he'd flown me to Port Station to get Luce and then back to The Middle when we couldn't find my craft.

"Because your residence in the canals was compromised."

I shook my head. "Not nearly good enough. You knew exactly where this place was. You shouldn't have that information. Where'd you get it?" When he didn't answer, I pressed the taser against his flesh, making an indent between the cords of his neck, while shoving the Gem into his forehead. Leaning over as far as I could, my lips almost touching his ear, I whispered, "If you don't tell me the truth, I'm gonna make it hurt."

"I paid for it."

"Paid who?" That was a mildly surprising answer. When he didn't respond, I ran my thumb over the taser trigger, exerting a teensy bit of pressure. It was enough to garner a spark—enough to make Case's muscles jump and seize for a quick second. That should be just the right amount.

"Some guy named Goliath at a skell a few blocks away," he panted.

I knew Goliath.

He owned that particular skell and was as big as a house, his face so adorned with carbon piercings and other markings that his natural skin tone was barely visible. It was meant to be intimidating, which worked in his favor.

He was no friend of mine.

It was unsurprising that Goliath knew I had a place somewhere around here—there would be talk. But I was a little perturbed he knew the exact location. I didn't buy it. "Goliath might have had a roundabout location, but you told me in the craft exactly where I should park. So either you're lying, or you spent time this morning scouring the buildings searching for my residence. Which is it?" Things didn't add up.

He cleared his throat, which was hard to do with my taser still pressed up snug against his thorax. "I thought you might be in danger, so I went looking for your place. Goliath knew where you lived. Said it wasn't a secret."

Shit. "What kind of danger?" By the tone of his admission, this was the serious kind of danger—the kind that got you killed, not just bruised or bloodied.

"If you back off, I'll tell you the rest of it." He ended on a grumble. I'd taken him completely off guard and gotten the best of him for the fourth time.

"You've already had a number of chances to confess. You flew me to Port Station this morning, and we just saw each other on the street. Honestly, Case, if you would've told me from the get-go that you were planning to spend the rest of the day stalking me, we could've handled this situation a lot differently from the start. For example, I would've just taken you down then. I don't bring people back to my residence. You've made me to break every single rule I have." Without his help, Daze would've died. I had to remember that. It was the only thing staying my hand at this point. That had earned him a short respite. For the next few minutes anyway.

Visibly gnashing his teeth, he snarled, "I wasn't *stalking* you. And I didn't have the information earlier, or else I would've warned you. I have no way to get a hold of you, since I don't have a tech phone. Finding your place seemed like the most logical place to start."

"Why not tell me on the street? You could've saved yourself a tase to the neck." I eased back a little bit, but not much.

"Then you wouldn't have brought me here."

True. "And what's so important that you had to accompany me here? It's not a safe practice to piss me off. I don't *trust* you." He had the nerve to grin. It wasn't a full smile with teeth, but a grin just the same. "What the hell is so funny?" His happiness made me incensed. I almost pulled the trigger again, this time a little harder.

"Goliath bet me I couldn't get in, even if I found the place. He said you'd kill me first."

"He's right," I said, not feeling at all mollified. "The only reason you're still breathing is it seems you have information to share—that may or may not save your life, depending on how stirring and informative it is." I stood. "Start sharing, Case, and it better be good. What kind of danger are we talking about? And why me?"

"It has to do with Tandor." He braced himself up on his elbows. I had both Gem and the taser still aimed at his smug face.

"Tandor?" We'd eradicated him. Specifically, my Gem had seared a hole through his belly, and he'd gone over a cliff with zero chance of survival.

Case began to rise, and I stepped back, allowing it. He got to his feet, rubbing his neck and making exaggerated motions with his chin. His neck muscles must be tight. Poor baby. "Remember when you asked me if any of Tandor's men would be a problem, even if we eliminated Tandor?"

"I do. We were in Seven and I hadn't yet realized you'd been double-crossing me for the second time. And now you're telling me there's a problem." I leaned against the wall.

"Not one, but two. I just found out this morning." He brushed his jacket off. Shit fell off. The floor was dirty. I didn't spend much time here, and cleaning wasn't a priority. He glanced around. "This is a pretty big space."

I absentmindedly followed his gaze, mulling over what he'd just told me. I'd had this place going on ten years. I shoved off from the wall and walked over, turning on some lights as I went. I wanted to see him better when he spilled the rest of the story. There were no openings to the outside in here. "It looks that way because all the internal walls are down. It's one big room, with a small waste area over there." I gestured to the right. "There's a crude sleeping cot in the corner and a small cooling unit next to it. It's bare bones. Enough small talk. What's going on with Tandor's men? And what does it have to do with the seeker I saw earlier?" I knew they were connected somehow.

Case made his way to one of two seats, and I headed to my cooling unit, passing a wall covered in batteries. That's what kept everything here powered. "There were survivors," he said once he sat, still massaging his neck. "One being Tandor's second in charge, Hutch, and a lackey who goes by the name of Slim. Slim was responsible for gathering the main objective for the group."

"Which was?"

"Procuring Plush."

Case had told me a little bit of Tandor's plan before the zealot had met his untimely end, but we'd been on the go and I hadn't internalized it, because I'd thought it wasn't going to matter once he was gone. "What were they planning on doing with the Plush?"

"Infect the masses."

I pulled up a chair after taking a jug of water out of the unit and holstering my taser. "I don't get it. What does that accomplish?" I upended the bottle and guzzled it, Bender style. It'd been a long morning, and I was hot and tired after exerting all that energy bringing Case to the ground. "Masses of seekers on the streets don't help a new government function. That can't be the end game. Why not just kill the unwilling citizens, instead of infect them?"

Case pulled off his helmet, his tousled brown hair sticking to the sides of his face. He ran a hand through it, mussing it up, his eyes focused on mine. "They want control, first and foremost. In order to get it, they're willing to dose people to keep any kind of rebellion to a minimum. They know a government overthrow will be difficult, at best. But I heard a rumor today that they might have a reversal at the ready to use after the takeover is complete."

"A reversal?" I set the water on the floor next to me, not offering any to Case. He'd have to ask.

"For the seekers."

I stilled for a moment before tugging off my own helmet. "You're talking about a *cure*, right?"

If it was true, then maybe there was an upside to all this crap after all.

Chapter 7

"Could be a cure," Case answered. "Nobody I talked to had exact information, just whispers about new seekers injected with Plush and it not necessarily being permanent."

"Why me?" I sat back in my chair, my gaze filled with suspicion, my Gem on my lap, the barrel aimed outward. "Why target me specifically?"

He shrugged. "You killed Tandor. You were also number one on Tandor's hit list. You're a known threat—you and your crew. Something that could make or break their success."

I thought back to the events of this morning, specifically Cozzi's fear about telling me what was going on and Ned's frantic request for protection in exchange for information.

Tracking Ned down would be next on my to-do list, after retrieving Luce and freeing Darby.

Based on Case's information, the setup Tandor used to dupe Darby just got a lot murkier. I stood. "You're going to sit tight while I gather up some things, and then we're out of here." I made my way to a large stack of supplies and salvages along the opposite wall from where we sat. There should be some reflective cloth here somewhere. I bent over, moving things around so I could get behind the first layer. "And, Case, don't think for a minute you're off the hook," I grumbled. "Everything you've said so far makes sense, but it doesn't explain it all, and I still haven't decided whether I'm going to inflict any more pain or not."

Footsteps sounded behind me. "I came here to warn you. Like I said."

I glanced over my shoulder, giving him a look that conveyed my feelings about his warning tactics. My eyelids couldn't get lower without fully closing, my lips pursed. "I told you to stay in your seat. You're pushing me too far. Goliath was right. You're messing with life-and-death stuff here." The problem was, a guy like Case didn't give a shit about that. He didn't live in fear of much. But it was in my best interests to keep reminding him.

Then, if he actually did die, my conscience would be clear.

Before Case could form a rebuttal, a beep sounded from my vest pocket. My tech phone was going off.

I stopped and pulled it out, depressing the button before speaking. "This is Ella."

"It's Jerry," Lockland said. "Change of plans. Need to

help my mother move some things. Will be unavailable until tomorrow."

My brows furrowed.

Shit.

He was talking about Claire. Something had come up that needed his immediate attention. That couldn't be good. I depressed the button again. "I hope she's okay." My heart began to race. Claire was a mother to all of us. "Need any help?"

"Johnny's with me. Should be enough."

"Keep me posted."

"Will do." Lockland's way of telling me he couldn't speak anymore.

Case read my face correctly. "Bad news?"

I glanced at him distractedly as I paced. "I'm not sharing anything with you, so don't ask." I spun in a circle. "How am I going to get Luce back?" Lockland and I were supposed to go get my craft at blackout.

Case stood in front of me, arms crossed. I was about to tell him to get lost when Bender's voice came out of the speaker in a growl, the phone still in my hand. "Breakfast tomorrow. Aaron should be with us." He cut out, the static disappearing, which meant he'd shut down, preventing further communication. I sat, my mind racing.

Aaron was Darby's handle.

Something was happening with Claire and Darby. Bender and Lockland had decided to act, likely within moments. I swore. I should've been there.

Case stood like a statue in the middle of the room,

which was irritating. But almost anything would piss me off right now. My family needed help, and I had no way to get to them. I made up my mind, heading toward the door, donning my helmet on the way. "Come on," I called, "we're leaving." I punched off the lights and had the door open before Case caught up.

"Where are we going?"

"We're going to get Luce. I can't do anything without my craft, and you owe me for the stunt you pulled to get up here, so you either agree, or I take Seven and do it myself." After he was out, I rigged the binder back in place, and brushed by him. "I'm flying."

Without comment, he walked around the craft to the passenger side.

I hit Seven's ignition button, but nothing happened. I sighed as I tilted my head against the rest. "Don't fuck with me, Case. We're in the middle of some serious stuff, and I need my craft."

"I agree," he said. "But going right now, in the middle of the day, isn't going to accomplish your goal."

"What are you suggesting?"

"Wait until blackout."

Lockland would've said something if he'd managed to secure a bribe by a guard at Port Station. Taking Luce back by force was the only viable option. Either that, or I snuck in, which was unlikely. "It won't make that much difference if it's dark or not. I'm going to have to take her at gunpoint either way. I don't know Port Station well enough to sneak in."

"I do."

My eyebrows rose. An offer of help would cost me. "What's the swap?"

"I want in on this."

"This what? Taking Hutch down?"

He nodded. "Yes. I want to see it to the end."

"Your sister and Tandor are gone. You got retribution for your nephew. Why not go back to where you came from?" I met his gaze head on, not surprised to see it held a hard edge. This man had a past. He was no saint. "You're not going home, are you?"

"No."

I sighed, this time taking my time with the exhale. I wasn't interested in why he'd chosen to stay. I wanted my craft back and my family safe, and I was willing to do a lot to make that happen, but I wasn't going to compromise anything on my end to get it. "Fine. You can tag along until I get Luce back, which will take until sometime tomorrow, but I'm not sharing any intel. That's all I'm offering."

"I want in until the end."

"Sorry, no can do," I said. "I reunite with my crew once they get back, and you're not invited. I can tell you about the seeker I saw and what went down, but that's all I have. Take it or leave it." He was about to counter my offer, judging by the look on his face and the tilt of his head, and I held up my hand. "I'm done negotiating. The offer stands."

"Done."

I waited a few seconds. "Are you going to engage the starter now and let me fly out of here?"

"It's already on."

Disbelieving, I hit the button again.

The propulsion fired immediately, and the craft bounced off the ground. Case hadn't moved. I would've seen it. I narrowed my eyes. He didn't meet my gaze. Instead, he seemed very interested in the twisted rafters outside the windshield. "You have a false start on this, don't you? What, it locks up every fifth time? Tricky bastard." Had I tried it again, I wouldn't have had to negotiate anything with him.

"No false start."

I jammed the left lever down, moving out fast, relishing watching Case's head whip forward as I reversed. "I don't believe you—"

An explosion rocked the space in front of us, as a pressure wave shot us backward, causing the craft to swoop and bounce. Thankfully, there was nothing behind us. I gripped the controls, barely managing to hold us steady. I'd just cleared the building, and if I hadn't been moving as quickly as I'd been, we would've been ripped apart.

Hands clasping the dash, Case shouted, "Get the hell out of here!"

"Working on it." I twisted the levers, arcing Seven one hundred and eighty degrees while still in reverse. If the Q7 hadn't been built for speed, this wouldn't have been possible. I accelerated us away, gunning the propulsion, the air displacement from the blast still causing massive turbulence in the form of shockwaves. My hands were like two iron vises on the levers. As I steadied us, I upped the speed to two hundred and fifty kilometers an hour.

When we were finally in the clear, I pounded a fist on the dashboard, punctuating each word. "They... just...blew...up...my fucking *house!*"

Case craned his neck to look behind us. "Thirty seconds sooner and we would've been dead."

I aimed the craft east, circling back just enough to watch the black smoke billowing up from what used to be my residence. The dark, acrid plumes were a cautionary reminder of what could've been. The blast had been concentrated, likely not disrupting the rest of the building. "That was a compact hydro-bomb meant for a contained explosion," I said. "My question is, how did they get it up there without me knowing? None of my traps had been tripped when we arrived."

"They must've used a launcher."

I shook my head as I maneuvered us toward the sea. "We would've heard something, and launchers leave vapor trails. That blast was local."

My residence was gone. Just like that. It was just fucking gone.

"It could've been on a timer," Case conceded.

"I don't think so. My guess is a wireless detonator. They weren't expecting me to accelerate out that quickly." The fact that someone had gotten up there and waited until we'd come back outside to activate was more than a little disconcerting—it was infuriating.

I'd found out about Tandor's arrival in my city a few days ago, and since then, my world had been completely rocked—and now blown sky high.

As I flew, my mind raced.

"Where are we headed?" Case asked.

"Back to the barracks," I said, distracted. "This explosion changes everything."

"Did you lose anything important back there?"

Important was code for *irreplaceable.*

"Yeah, my damn peace of mind." I'd been living and surviving in this city for twenty-seven years, mostly on my own, and had never lost so much in a single event. "Back there was a culmination of years' worth of salvaging. These guys are going to pay for what they did. That was my life, the way I make my living." If they blew up my canals residence, I'd have to start over. I had a small residence near Government Square, but that was just for show. An address to give out if I was ever arrested. The thought wasn't very appealing—it actually bordered on horrifying.

"They made a mistake," Case said.

"Are you kidding me?" I almost shrieked, my heart beating rapidly in my chest. "The only mistake they made was not killing me."

He shook his head. "No, I mean they left us a trail."

"What trail?"

He turned in his seat, his helmet in his lap. "The only one who saw us take off together and could give them any solid information was the guy I paid on the roof to watch my craft."

I thought back to that surly old man. He'd retreated fairly quickly. It was possible he had a tech phone in his possession and whoever he was communicating with had to be someplace close-by. "So we get that guy to talk, find out who paid him, and track these assholes down."

"The sooner the better."

"We can't do it now. This area's hot. It needs to cool down before we head back. And when we find them, I might blow their shit up. Just for the fun of it." I steered Seven toward the ocean. "I mean, fair's fair."

Chapter 8

"Kid," I said, rubbing a temple, "I don't think I heard you correctly. Say it again." Daze being happy to see us was an understatement. He was thankfully feeling better, and by the time we'd arrived back at the bunker, he'd been literally bouncing off the walls. The medi-pod, it seemed, had fixed his ailments. He was almost completely healed, at least by outward appearances.

Daze held a bag of prepackaged food a meter from my face, shaking it proudly. Dried, pale flakes bounced around inside. "I found these. They were way back in the corner. I dug them out. They're really old, but you can still eat them. It says to add hot water. Nobody would've found them if I hadn't been here." He tilted his chin up in the classic Daze pose. "They were tucked deep inside a hole in the wall. I think somebody was trying to save them for later. You wouldn't have even seen it. You're too tall."

"Yeah, that's great, but what did you say about the

pico again? That's the part I need." I was reclined on one of the two couches, focusing my mind on a solid plan for tonight. Getting Luce back was imperative. Then we had to deal with the old man.

On the way back to the barracks, I'd tried to get a hold of Bender and Lockland, but neither answered. I was beginning to worry—not the fretting kind of worry, but the kind that settled in your gut like a heavy stone. Only a severe emergency would've caused the guys to leave without me. I was an asset, not a liability. Whatever was happening with Claire and Darby, it was something that couldn't wait.

That was never good.

Daze plopped down on the couch across from me, the bag still clutched in his fist. Case was in the waste room at the back of the massive space that made up the barracks. "I said I really have a pico. I told Tandor my dad used to have one but that he took it with him when he left. But it was a lie." Daze's face was intense as he relayed the story. "I convinced Tandor that telling you I had one would be enough to get you to go to Port Station. But I really did have one. He didn't know I'd taken the quantum drive yet. Isn't that cool?" He was momentarily distracted by the flakes as he gave the bag another shake, examining the contents two centimeters from his eyeballs.

I hadn't been able to quiz Daze on everything that had happened. He'd been near death after I'd shot Tandor and had still been groggy this morning. This was our first official debriefing.

I sat up, unfurling from my reclined position, my mind now at rock-solid attention. "Yes, that's super cool. Your brain is big and vast. But you're going to have to back up a bit more. How and where do you have this pico?" Getting pertinent info out of Daze before Case came back had just become a big priority. I wasn't interested in sharing with the outskirt. In fact, I wasn't inclined to divulge anything I didn't have to, even though I'd agreed he could help me. I didn't trust him. How did I know for sure he wasn't behind the bomb that blew up my house? It was a little miraculous that we'd gotten out just in time. And in my world, miracles didn't happen.

"It's back at my residence," he answered, like it was no big deal. *Shake, shake.* Full examination of the flakes once again.

"Like, as in the place I was at in Port Station two days ago, the one where I almost got killed?"

"Yep." He finally set the bag on the table between us, angling his head to look around the room, searching for the next thing that could captivate his attention.

I wanted it to be this conversation.

Crossing my arms, I made my voice stern. "Is it under the stairs like you told me?"

"Nope. It's under my bed. In the floor. I put it there real careful before I left. I had to go, you know, because my mom died." His mouth slid down into a frown as he stared at the floor, his toes barely touching the ground, his shoes making intermittent scuffing sounds as he kicked them back and forth.

I had to keep reminding myself he was just a twelve-year-old kid. A child interested in playing games and having fun.

"And you're sure Tandor had no idea you had one?" I asked. "You didn't brag to anyone else about it? Not even Rennie?" His friend Renata had been used as a pawn in Tandor's game to get Daze to cooperate. I was pretty sure she was dead, but nobody had confirmed it, and there wasn't an easy way to find out.

His gaze met mine, his chin beginning to tilt upward. "I didn't brag. None of the runaways would know what it was anyway. I told Renata that I had some cool stuff, but not what it was. We were just goofing around one day, and she told me she hid stuff, too."

I stood. "Well, that settles it, then. I'm heading back to your place tonight before I pick up Luce." My face was set as I addressed the kid one more time. "You're not sending me on a wild-goose chase again, are you?" That was a nice way of saying Daze was a talented actor. I'd fallen for everything he'd dished, thoroughly and completely. If I thought about it too hard, I'd get pissed again, and that wouldn't help either of us. "Because if you are, things will get tricky between us really quick."

Instead of taking offense at my stern tone, Daze bounced up and down on the couch on his butt, his hands braced by his sides, a look of excitement on his face. "I can go with! I'll show you where it is. I promise it's there. It's not a lie. Tandor was a bad guy. He forced me to do things I didn't want to do. But not anymore. Because you killed him." He smiled widely, his eyes bright and adoring, like I'd slain his personal dragon—which I kind of had. Daze abruptly stilled, a serious look sweeping over his features. "I promise never to lie to you again." The kid actually placed a hand over his heart. "If I do, may seekers rip my heart out and eat it until I die."

"Ew, that would be a terrible way to go." I chuckled. Behind us, Case exited the waste room. In a hurried tone, I whispered, "Okay, I believe you. But you can't come with because it's too dangerous." I didn't want to tell him that Tandor's men could still be out there. It was too soon to freak him out. "And kid, we're keeping this to ourselves for now. Catch my drift?" I angled my head toward the footsteps heading toward us, giving Daze a pointed look.

His face changed to something that resembled cunning in the space of a single second. "I understand." Daze snatched the bag of food off the tech table and darted off, bounding up to Case, shaking it. "Look what I found! It was hidden real good. I found a bunch of them, all different flavors." He bounced up and down. "This one says it's chicken-soup flavored, whatever that is. Can we try it?"

Oh, that kid was more than a talented actor. He was smooth.

It was almost astounding how well he played the game. I'd have to remember going forward that it could be a big mistake not to take him seriously.

Case led him over to the cooling unit and withdrew

some water. Then he reached into a drawer for an ultrasonic whisk. Once inserted into the cup, it would heat the molecules instantly. Daze gleefully tore off the top of the package, chatting nonstop about some nonsense.

As they worked, I made my way back to the waste room. It was my turn to shower. When I was finished, I emerged to find Daze waiting with a bowl full of something brown and murky. As I moved closer, he held it out to me. "The other one was gross, but this one is okay. It's mushy, but good." I took the proffered food and ate, thankful for something that had a different flavor and texture than what I was used to. My taste buds were surprised by the new taste and let my brain know, but I didn't have any labels for the specific food it was supposed to mimic, because I hadn't ever sampled it before. "It's…interesting, I'll give it that," I said between bites. When I was done, I walked it over to the trash bin.

Back in the day, a good garbage compactor would break down the waste for compost and recycling, separating it by atomic weight and sending the pieces down separate chutes. The best we could hope for now was an even grind.

I turned back to find Case staring at me.

He'd showered. His hair was still a little damp, sticking up where he'd haphazardly run his fingers through it. His stubble was gone, which meant he'd used a blade or had access to a micro-follicle laser. Either way, his jaw was clean and looked a little more prominent without its usual coating. "When are we leaving to get your craft?" he asked.

"Not sure," I said. "Definitely after blackout, but I'm thinking we should wait until the early hours. Less guards on duty."

He nodded. "I agree. But I think we should pay the guy on the roof a visit before we head to Port Station. We need information while the trail is still warm, and they won't be expecting us to come back so soon."

I leaned my hips back against the edge of the counter next to the bin and crossed my arms. "And what makes you think the old guy's still there? If I were him, I wouldn't stick around."

Case shrugged. "He lives there. Where else would he go?"

That was a valid point.

It was likely better to try to track him down now rather than later. "Okay, fine, we'll head there first, but we go after midnight." I walked toward the couches. "I still can't believe they blew my place up. All of it is gone. Just gone." I shook my head as I sat. In the scope of things, losing this residence was hard, but not impossible to recover from. I had supplies littered all over the city. It would just take time to round it all up. And I was alive. There was always that.

"Who blew up your place?" Daze asked, his expression confused as he came to sit next to me. I hadn't mentioned anything, but it would be hard to keep this kind of information from the kid in the long run, so just telling him was the best choice.

"It seems the bad guys are still in town," I said. "But before you get too excited, they can't get us here. We're super protected."

"Tandor's guys." Daze's voice was glum. His head pitched downward as he swung his feet around. "They had a bunch of Plush, and they were always trying to get more. I knew they'd survive. They didn't like Tandor."

I squinted at the kid. He was full of surprises. "What do you know about it?"

Daze's eyebrows furled in concentration. He was quiet for a few seconds. "They didn't think I was listening, but I always was. Sometimes, I pretended to be asleep. Other times, I hid under a desk. They're going to use Plush on everyone," he blurted, his voice quavering. "They said it would control the resisters better, so they could take over with less people getting in their way. They called everyone 'sheep' and 'stupid,' then they'd laugh. They were evil."

My gaze met Case's, and we shared a look. "If they're going to infect everyone with Plush, how will they control all the new seekers?" I asked Daze. "You saw how they acted when they attacked us after we crossed that beam. They're mindless. You'd think it would be a big headache to have a bunch more seekers getting in the way of their plans." It didn't make much sense to me, anyway.

"They have this ancidote," Daze whispered, like it was a secret. "It calms them down. Tandor said he wanted to use some of them as slaves."

"I think you mean antidote," I corrected. I addressed Case. "I saw Dill shove a dart in the seeker's forehead, then she collapsed in his arms. I didn't stick around to see what happened next, but what the kid's saying sounds right. They definitely have something."

Case stood in front of Daze. "Who do you think is running things now? Did you know Tandor's men very well? Would you recognize them if you saw them again?"

Daze's head bobbed up and down. "The really bad guy was Hutch. If he's still alive, he would be in charge." The kid's tone couldn't get much drearier. Guessing he was not a fan of this Hutch guy. "He's really ugly, and he has a scar on his face." Daze slashed his index finger down the side of his right cheek. "I heard him talking about killing Tandor one time. He said he was 'a useless piece of shit.' Hutch always had one guy with him. His name was Slim, but we called him Slime. He was always sneaking around doing things behind Tandor's back."

It seemed I'd been right in my original assumption that Tandor had run a sloppy organization. This Hutch guy must've known that we'd defeat Tandor in the end. My guess was he hadn't been at the gorge for the showdown on purpose. I would've remembered someone with a scar. "What does Slim look like?" I asked.

"He looks regular," Daze said, shrugging, his feet beginning to scuff along the floor again. We'd have to work on his attention spanning more than five minutes at a time.

"And what does *regular* mean, exactly?"

Daze popped off the seat. "He looks like everybody else." Reaching his quota of talk, he took off toward the back of the room, likely in search of more hidden food stashes.

Case cleared his throat after the kid bounded away. "He thinks all adults look the same."

"I'm going to have to teach him how to remember even the most mundane details, but it's going to take time. I guess we're just going to have to go with regular for now."

Case took water out and set it on the counter. Then he got out a cup and poured himself a glass. "The kid was likely in panic mode most of the time. I'm not surprised he can't tell any of them apart."

"You know their names," I said as I stood. "How come you don't know what they look like?"

Case downed the liquid. "Because I never bothered to ask my informant."

"That's convenient."

"Why would I need to know what Tandor's henchmen looked like?"

"When I heard your sister talking by the gorge, it seemed like you knew a few of them personally. One guy said that after she killed her kid, they couldn't trust you anymore, but why would they have trusted you in the first place? Lots of things don't add up, Case. But you know that already."

"I did know a few people." He braced his back against the cooling unit, his expression bland, no telltale tic by his eye. "That's how I met my informant. But they were only people who hung around with my sister, the ones recruited from my tribe. She wasn't well-liked. Tandor kept his inner circle close, and it seemed he had good reason if he was dealing in Plush."

I grunted as I walked toward the sleeping pods. Case had answered without answering—his typical runaround. "I'm going to get an hour or two of shut-eye before we go. I want to be rested for this." What I didn't say was that I was antsy as hell and was going to use the time to plot by myself. I didn't want Case's input or interference. Not knowing his angle bugged me.

As I climbed into the pod I'd used last night, Daze came charging at me. "Look what I found!" It appeared to be the same exact bag as before. "There was another stash." His voice was brimming with excitement. "This place is crawling with hidey-holes!"

I nodded as I lay back. "This can only mean one thing."

"That I'm good at finding things?"

"Yep, which means you're going to make an excellent salvager." His chest puffed. "Listen," I said in a conspiratorial tone, "while Case and I are gone, I'm going to need you to search every millimeter of this space and see what you can find." I lodged my arm behind my head as a pillow. "Since they blew my house up, I'm going on a full recon mission to recoup what I've lost. I bet you can find a bunch of supplies here. After you're done, get some sleep. We'll most likely be back by daybreak. If for some reason we don't come back right away, I don't want you to panic. You have more than enough stuff here"—I nodded toward the bag in his hand—"to keep you alive for a long time. If we're not back in a week, you pack a big bag of supplies and head northwest." I pulled a tech phone out of my vest pocket. "I want you to have this." I set it in his hand. His eyes widened. "It won't work in here because the walls are too thick, but as you get closer to the city, reach out to Bender and Lockland. Do you remember your handle and the channels we use?"

He nodded solemnly, stuffing the tech phone deep in his front pants pocket. "But...but you're coming back, right? I won't need to do all that." I could hear the fear just under the surface.

"That's the plan, kid. But we know life doesn't always work the way we want it to. I'm going to have Case show you how to get out of this place if you need to. You're going to have to use tools to get the main door open, but as I said, it's only precautionary. If we don't plan for the worst, we get caught with our pants down, and we don't want that. Life without pants would be difficult. Are we clear?"

"Clear."

"Cheer up," I said, observing his drawn face. I playfully bumped a fist against his shoulder. "We're still alive. That's a win right there. We'll take care of Hutch and Slim, just like we did Tandor. Have no fear. Nobody messes with my city and gets away with it."

"Holly?"

"Yeah?"

"Can I sleep next to you? Just for a little bit?" His voice cracked. "I mean, I don't have to…I can go look for stuff—"

Careful to conceal my surprise, I kept a straight face as I answered, "Sure. Come on in." I slid over to make room, patting the area next to me. "You've had a rough few days. It looks like you could use a little rest. I didn't want to say anything before, but sleep is a smart option."

His face was filled with relief as he climbed in. "Thanks. I promise once I get up, I'll search real careful for everything."

"I know you will." I didn't have to look at Case to know he'd heard it all. "After some sleep, you'll be ready for anything." He curled up next to me, his back tucked into my side. I tentatively laid an arm over him and heard him sigh. His breathing evened out in less than two minutes. The kid must've been stressed waiting for us to come back. Footsteps neared. I glanced up at the outskirt. "Give us three hours."

He nodded once and lowered the lid.

It took me a lot longer than the kid to fall asleep.

Chapter 9

"Are you sure you can find the location without your running lights on?" I asked Case, who was piloting Seven. I was skeptical. Operating a dronecraft with no lights during blackout was tricky at best, but in a city you were unfamiliar with, even more so. But he'd insisted on flying, and since I would have had to pull my Gem to argue, I let it go. We were on our way to question the old man on the roof.

"Yes."

"Completely sure?" Flying after blackout wasn't common. We would be noticed, because drones weren't exactly quiet. We had to achieve our mission quickly, and to do so, the pilot needed to know their way around. "All the buildings look similar in the dark."

"I got it." Case was intently focused, his eyes locked on the view in front of us through the windshield.

"You know, if I was the questioning kind, which I am, I'd think you were more familiar with this city than you let on." Case grunted, dropping altitude suddenly, causing me to reach for the dash. I'd smartly strapped myself in upon entry. "That's not an efficient way to shut me up. You'll have to do more—"

The craft lurched, spinning quickly at a ninety-degree angle. My arms shot out to brace myself, one of which landed on Case's shoulder. He chuckled as he evened out. "Sorry about that. Hard to see in between these buildings. It's dark out."

"Very funny." My pulse had sped up more than I would've liked, and my breathing hitched. "Okay, so you've found a way to shut me up for a total of one minute. Happy? But that doesn't mean you win. The only victory you get will be when you land us on the roof in one piece."

"I'm not landing on the roof."

"What? How else are we going to get there?" A roof landing would be the fastest way to achieve our goals. We wanted to question this guy and get the hell out. I still had to get Luce and retrieve the pico before daybreak. Port Station was a twenty-minute flight from here.

"Because I want to take him by surprise, if we can," Case replied. "He could have a tech phone or a locator. We don't want to give him a chance to use them."

"That's true, he could, especially if he's being paid by Tandor's men," I retorted. "But even if he had time to use it before we stormed his tin shack, they'd have to arrive before we take off. I'm planning on this requiring no more than three minutes of our time, five, tops."

Case directed the craft up, gaining altitude. "Do you really think you can get him to talk that fast?"

"Yes indeed."

"He has more to lose by talking to you. Once they find out he's a rat, they'll kill him."

"My methods are tried and true. I can get a confession out of someone quicker than a dose of Babble. Have no fear." Case didn't shrug, but he might as well have. "You don't believe me?"

"No, I do."

"Yeah, right. I can tell by the tone of your voice you think I'm lying. But watch and learn. I'll have a confession out of him in less than three minutes, and we'll be out in five. Land on the roof. No one can get to him that quickly, even if he signals for help."

"We won't get a second chance," he warned.

"I'm not looking for one," I said, irritation leaking through. What else did this guy need? A signed document? "Trust me. Land on the roof." The passenger window wasn't positioned to give me the view I needed, so I had to put faith that he was steering us in the right direction. Case headed left, and gradually, I began to pick out familiar surroundings. "There it is." I pointed. "Up ahead three buildings on the right." Case ignored my helpful directions and instead veered left.

I waited to see what he was up to, managing to keep my mouth shut.

After a few more turns, he dropped to roofline level, inching closer to our destination. At an intersection, he zoomed straight up, gaining altitude with the aid of a hydro-booster, the telltale whooshing noise of the spent canister giving it away.

Once we were high in the air, he centered us over the building, then killed the motors, stopping the props.

Then he did something I'd never seen before.

He engaged a different hydro-boost, but this one aimed downward, cushioning us in a rush of air as we dropped.

"Case, how are you going to land like this—"

A moment before impact, he hit the props and the landing gear at the same time. We bounced up a few meters before making a graceful, quiet landing on the roof.

I didn't have time to compliment his excellent piloting skills, because I was out of the craft, using our advantage just as I'd promised. Tugging my Gem and taser out, I raced for the cobbled-together lean-to in the corner where the old man had scurried the last time we'd seen him. There was a piece of sheet metal covering the opening. I kicked it in. It flew inward, landing with a clatter. I raced over it, pulling up short, momentarily confused by the scene in front of me.

Case was behind me half a beat later, stopping to assess the situation over my shoulder. "I think it's safe to say he won't be sharing anything with us, no matter how stellar your interrogation skills are."

"You're right about that." I holstered my guns and moved cautiously to the old man's side. His neck had been slashed—and not all that long ago, judging by the consistency of the blood. Small trickles of red still dribbled out of the wound, but most of it had congealed, covering his front like a sticky, wet blanket. I nudged his shoulder. His head flopped forward, landing at an awkward angle. "Shit. What are we going to do now?" I glanced around the small space, searching for clues. I picked up and examined a few of his meager possessions, setting them back down when they didn't reveal any pertinent information. Too bad miscellaneous junk couldn't talk.

Case gently laid the old man back into a resting position, patting him down, inspecting his pockets. "They took him by surprise. He would've fought it if he'd seen it coming, but there are no signs of resistance." Case unfurled one of the man's closed fists, and three coins dropped out.

"They paid him," I said, "then killed him. In the end, he was a liability if we came back."

Propellers sounded nearby. Case grabbed my arm and spun us around. "We're getting out of here now."

"I'm right behind you," I said. We'd both left the doors to the craft lofted. Within a meter of Seven, I vaulted off the ground, landing in the passenger seat, my arm simultaneously bringing the door down to secure it as Case did the same. "I hope you didn't burn out all your hydro-boosts getting here. Because we're going to need them."

Whoever was coming after us would give chase, and by the sound of the propellers, they were almost on top of us.

Case accelerated as the craft darted in behind us. It

wasn't familiar to me, and I made it my business to know many of the crafts in the city. "Strap yourself in," he grunted. "It's going to be a rough ride."

I had already tugged my arms through the straps. "One step ahead of you." I buckled in, leaning forward as far as I could. "I know how to ditch them. This neighborhood is full of wasted buildings. Follow my instructions, and we should be able to lose them." It was going to be a bitch to do it in the dark, but we didn't have any choice. "Up ahead at that intersection, take a right." I gestured out the windshield. "One block down, left. There will be a building on your right with a hole running through the middle. There's a steel beam that juts down halfway through. When I say dip, do it. The likelihood of our pursuers knowing it's there is highly unlikely. If they follow, they crash."

Case did as I directed. They were tailing us, but they weren't gaining.

"Here?" Case asked, strumming with tension.

My head whipped around. "Yes, go," I urged, gripping the dash as he whipped the craft into the building. In my head, I counted to two. "Dip!" Seven fell effortlessly, regaining herself in the next instant. There was a slight grating sound running along the roof—Case had successfully skimmed the beam, but it'd been close. I turned to watch for the other craft. It wasn't behind us. I turned to Case, confused. "They didn't follow us in."

Seven exited out the other side, and Case veered east, keeping low. "The monitor is clear. There's no craft in the area." He was right. No red blinking light, no beep.

That meant they were already more than a few kilometers away. They'd either gone back the other way, or they'd landed and switched off power. No matter what, it was confusing. They'd had us in their sights. Why not come after us? "I don't understand." I craned my head around one more time to be sure. "Why wouldn't they give chase?"

"Maybe we had it wrong," he answered casually. "Maybe we caught them off guard, and they were coming back from doing something else when they encountered us."

"Or maybe they recognized your craft and backed the fuck off." My voice held all the pent-up anger cascading through my body. I was getting sick of this. Trusting this guy was impossible.

"I'm no friend of theirs." His hands gripped the controls tightly. "The old guy would've told them we were together. That implicates me."

"It doesn't implicate you if you're *actually* on their side," I said. "None of this adds up." Frustration didn't come close. "Once I get Luce and pick up the kid, we go our separate ways. I'm done with this bullshit."

"I'm not lying to you." His jaw clenched. "I'm not colluding with them. I have no idea why they didn't follow us."

Case could be telling the truth, or he could be lying. There was no way to tell for sure, and based on his past record, it could swing either way. "It was your idea to go back and question the old guy, exactly at this time. It was convenient for him to have been killed moments before we arrived. Then to have a craft waiting to spy on us? It doesn't add up, no matter what you say." I faced forward in my seat, my spine straight. "If I hadn't been with you, maybe my residence would still be in one piece."

"Maybe."

My gaze shot toward his. "What's that supposed to mean? Are you admitting your guilt? That would be a first."

He snorted. It was a raspy, masculine sound that rang of self-assurance. "All I'm saying is that if you hadn't gone up to the roof with me, there's a possibility your place wouldn't have been blown up," he clarified. "When the old man saw us together, he could've tipped them off. If you remember correctly, I almost got killed as well. Even if I was in league with them, which I'm not"—he cut me off before I could argue that point—"I wouldn't risk dying over it."

"Why not? Maybe what they've offered is too enticing for you to pass up. The risks are high, but the payoff is *unbelievable*."

"Like what? What would be worth dying for? If I'm not breathing, I can't very well partake in a big reward."

I gave him a look, but he probably couldn't see it because it was dark and we were flying without lights. "I don't know. How about wealth, or your own passel of seeker-slaves, or a chance to dominate the city?

Power is addictive. If this Hutch guy has it to give, why wouldn't you take his offer? The bomb could've been intended as a near miss. After all, we survived."

He chuckled, which made me fume. "Yeah, a harem of seeker-slaves and world domination in this shitty place. That sounds enticing. Definitely worth dying over."

I crossed my arms and slouched in my seat, mumbling, "People have betrayed their fellow man for less."

Chapter 10

We were entering Port Station on foot.

Case had insisted, and since he was flying, there had been no other choice but for me to follow once he'd landed Seven outside the area. He'd argued that the Port Station guards wouldn't be expecting an attack without a craft. He also knew exactly where to head, which just added to my suspicions that this man couldn't be trusted.

"How did you know this way in again?" I asked for the second time. I was trying to whisper, but it was tiresome, and there was no one around. At least not for another kilometer or so. I hadn't decided how I was going to ditch Case to get the pico on my own. I'd figure that out once we arrived.

"I already told you," he said. "This is how I came in the first time. I paid one of the guards to give me a way in. People are easy to bribe, if you know where to find them."

"When I first encountered you"—*encountered* was a nice way of saying *when you shoved me out a two-story window*—"Seven was parked inside the city limits. You did not come through this opening on foot."

"I came in to scout the night before."

The area we walked through was dense with old, broken trees that finally gave way to a row of short brick buildings that hadn't been updated since before the dark days, judging by their dilapidated state. They were unoccupied and would be hazardous to anyone's health, the roofs caving in, their sides bowing precariously inward.

Just past them sat the wall that ran around the small city.

I could see the crack from here. It was big enough for a body to slip through, nothing more.

"Dammit," I muttered as we eased through, entering Port Station.

"What?" Case asked.

"Nothing." As luck would have it, we were standing at the end of Daze's block. His shallow apartment unit sat proudly in the middle of the street. I hadn't expected us to come in so close. I had to make a decision. Grabbing Case's arm, I suggested, "How about we split up? We can cover more ground that way."

It was dark, and we both had our visors down. I could see the look on his face through infrared, since he stood only a few centimeters away. It was confusion mixed with curiosity. "What are you talking about?" he said. "We need to stay together and find your craft."

I hedged. "I think we can do it better separately." I tried to sound convincing, adding in some matter-of-fact inflections. "That way, if one of us encounters trouble, the other will still have a chance to get Luce."

If he could've taken the time to cross his arms, he would have. "What am I missing here? Nothing should be more important than getting the quantum drive back at this point."

Well, what good was having a quantum drive if you had no pico to read it on?

That was tempting to say out loud, but I settled on, "I just think it's better to split up."

He shook his head. "We're only going to get one chance to get your craft, and if they start shooting, us both being there gives us better odds."

"Fine." I gritted my teeth. "But I have one stop to make before we go, no questions asked. I go alone." Before he could try to broker a deal with me, I took off, hugging close to the shadows, keeping an ear out for any trouble. Case moved quietly behind me.

I pulled up in front of the trash bin that I'd stuffed Daze behind a couple of nights ago. It was overturned, and I had to ease around the mound of garbage to get to the front door. Case had to recognize where we were. "Stay here," I whispered as I made my way up the front steps. Immediately, footfalls echoed behind me. I spun around. "What are you doing? I told you to stay."

With a straight face, Case said, "I can help you get the pico."

My eyes narrowed. "What makes you think I'm after something like that?"

"I thought you might be going after the supercomputer tucked in the floorboards under the kid's mattress."

"How the hell did you know what I was coming for?" I whisper-yelled as I stepped over the threshold, allowing the outskirt to follow me inside. I felt like shoving him up against the wall by his lapels, but instead, I stayed on task.

"I overheard you talking to Daze back at the bunker. I thought coming into Port Station this way would make things easier."

Now it was time to act. I slid my taser out of my waistband as I turned, getting in Case's face, causing him to take a step backward, his shoulders hitting the wall behind us. The fingers of my free hand tiptoed up his chest, my voice calm and steady. "It would be physically impossible for you to overhear us from all the way in the back of the barracks. How many voice recorders do you have set up?" When he didn't answer speedily, I brought my other hand up and placed the taser against his neck. Now, Case was a big guy, at least a head taller than I am, and much thicker. He could've overpowered me if he wanted to. But I'd also gotten the best of him quite a few times and could discharge the taser before he could fully dislodge me. I sensed his weariness and indecision.

"Three," he finally admitted. "And they're not recorders, they're amplifiers."

When was I going to learn? Apparently, never. The worst part was, I would've done the same thing. I'd fallen victim to yet another thing I hadn't bothered to consider. "I haven't noticed an earpiece." Amplifiers required the person listening in to have an ear device. He reached into his front pocket and pulled out a small clear tube. I leaned over to inspect it. It was an incredibly rare amplifier, something crafted just before the dark days. It was made of pliable elastomer and was meant to be molded into your inner ear canal. I'd seen only one other in my lifetime. In a government office. The one I used was bigger, and plainly obvious to anyone who was paying attention. I shoved both my hands against his chest, angry at my lack of foresight, and took a step back. "The rules of trust include not spying on each other. But then, you haven't been truthful with me since the very first moment I met you, so I don't know why I'm surprised. It's my fault for not assuming you were listening the entire time." I narrowed my gaze. "I better not have a tracker in me."

"No tracker."

I started up the stairs. "You're hacking away at any amount of trust we've built in the last few days by constantly sneaking around."

"We've built trust?" He sounded genuinely surprised.

"Er…no," I conceded, frustrated. Listening for a threat and having a conversation with the outskirt wasn't the best idea. "But if we had, it would be totally destroyed right now."

He followed me closely, his voice dropping low. "If I wanted the pico for myself, or had been in contact with Tandor's men, I would've found a way to part ways with you hours ago to retrieve it. When we arrive upstairs, and the pico is still where Daze said it would be, you'll know I'm being honest."

"We'll see." Once inside Daze's apartment, I headed straight to the bedroom. I hoisted up the stained mattress that Daze had spent his first eleven years on and tossed it aside. Kneeling on the floor, I flipped up my visor, tapping both shoulder lights on so we could see.

"Here, use this." Case handed me a long, thin piece of graphene with a curve at the end. He must have some deep pockets in that trench.

I stuffed the modified tool into a crack in the wood, testing for a loose board. It was amazing the wood hadn't decayed beyond recognition after all this time. About twenty years before the dark days, wood had been coated with a strong, newly invented polymer coating. It hardened to a superstrong finish. But even that had eroded in most places over the last sixty years.

After my third try, I found what I needed and the board came up easily. I set it aside and did the same to the one next to it.

Case and I both leaned over, gazing into the newly exposed opening.

It was empty.

I was just about to draw my Gem when Case edged

me out of the way, dropping to his stomach as he dipped his arm into the hole. A scraping noise followed, and I held my breath. He tugged something out.

It was much smaller than I'd anticipated. No bigger than twenty centimeters square. "That's it?" I was skeptical.

Case handed it to me. "I would assume. I've never seen one before."

I turned it over in my hands before sliding it down the front of my vest. Now was not the time to investigate. We had to get out of here. "Double-check to see if there's anything else down there. I promised Daze we'd get it all."

Case reached down and came back with a small box, something that looked to be a carbon pen, and an old action figure of some kind. Before the dark days, the toy industry had been huge. Literature and movies had accompanying merchandise. Since making a movie was easy, as was procuring a 3-D printer to make toys in mass quantities, the market had been saturated with both. A movie could be directly uploaded into people's homes, for a nominal fee, the moment it was finished. The screen in my home in the canals would've been used for that purpose.

Books had been similar. They could be uploaded to any device, and you could pick any voice you wanted to narrate, even someone famous. Or you could read at your leisure from anyplace in your home that had a screen, including your cooling unit. Children's books had come with a choice of stable or animated. The entertainment industry had been a vast money-making empire that had consistently and effectively adapted to ever-changing technology.

Without being asked, Case tucked Daze's possessions into his coat pocket.

We headed back down the stairs. I was almost to the front door when a figure stepped out from a doorway on my right, holding what looked to be a metal rod. My weapons were already drawn, my shoulder lights illuminating the face of a middle-aged woman dressed in a raggedy outfit.

She waved her meter-long piece of silvery titanium back and forth in a menacing way, like she was trying to ward off an evil spirit. "What are you doing?" she clucked. "You don't belong here!"

"Tell me about it," I muttered, forced to stop and deal with the situation, rather than just leave. "We're just passing through."

"What did you get up in there?" She spoke in a heavy accent. So much so, I almost couldn't understand her. It sounded close to *whadja git a en der.* It was a pidgin form of English that many people outside the city limits used. She'd likely never ventured away from Port Station. "The kid and his mama lived in that unit. Whatever is theirs is mine." I strained to make out her exact words, but the meaning was clear: She wanted what we had.

Was she honestly coming up against my firepower, aimed solidly at her midsection, with a tube? Did I not look intimidating enough in my synthetic leather, gloves, helmet, and boots? This woman wore a government uniform that had been pieced together, sewn into some sort of housecoat.

She swung the rod at me.

I had to hop back to avoid it, which pissed me off. I didn't have time for this. "Whoa, lady. Have you seen these things I'm holding?" I wiggled my hands to draw attention to my weapons. She honestly couldn't miss them. "I can do a hell of a lot more damage than that piece of hollow titanium, especially since I know how to use them real good." I ended the last bit in pidgin, so it sounded like *sin I ken use dem ril gud.* Just to make sure she understood me and there was no gray area.

"Your fancy-ass shit doesn't impress me. I want my stuff."

My eyebrows rose.

This had to be a joke. Bad people with access to bombs just blew up my entire residence. I sensed Case's laughter behind me. But instead of tasing her and being done with it, I leaned forward and asked curiously, "How do you know the boy who lived upstairs?"

"His mama and me were close." *He mam en my wire closs.*

Huh. *You don't say, lady.* "Were you by chance the boy's sustainer after his mother passed?" I didn't add *the one who was going to sell him into slavery.*

"Yeah, that was me. Now give me my stuff back." She swung the tube again.

This time, I didn't flinch.

"That's not going to happen." I took a step forward, my face hardening into my special *don't fuck with me* look. "Not only is it *not* your stuff, but I have a few issues with your sustainer values. Was it true that you were going to sell Daze into slavery for a few quick coins?" My voice was ramping up toward rage. Anyone with two brain cells to rub together would've taken a step back.

But this lady must be short a cell or two.

She stood there looking obtuse. "The kid was a pain in the ass. Nothing but a complainer." Her words were even harder to understand when she spoke quickly. "Slavery would've hardened him up, got him ready for life on the outside."

No need to hear any more.

Lifting my foot, and with very little effort on my part, I connected the sole of my boot with her stomach. She uttered a satisfying *oof* as she plummeted backward, the metal rod jerking out of her hand, landing on the floor with a sharp clatter. She hit the wall and half fell, half slouched her way down. Once on the ground, she remained unmoving, which was the only smart thing she'd done since she stepped into the hallway waving her ridiculous weapon.

"I hear you have another kid," I said as I moved closer. When she didn't answer, I lifted my foot again.

Her arms lofted into the air. "I have one. He's a good boy!"

I squatted next to her so we were on the same level. There would be no mistaking my intent. "If I hear one word about you harming that kid or selling him into slavery, I will hunt you down, and you will beg for mercy. Are we clear?" The lights from my shoulders bathed her face in blue. Her eyes were wide, her expression fearful.

"I love that boy. I would never harm him." *I la dat buoy. I ould nay hirm he.*

I stood. "Then we're all good." On the way out, I called over my shoulder, "And don't even think about placing one skinny leg inside that unit upstairs. It's mine."

Chapter 11

Case didn't comment on what had happened with housecoat lady on our way to the guard station, which was fine by me. It'd felt great to avenge Daze. I imagined the kid's response when I told him the story, his eyes shining, a smile full of teeth, and a quippy rebuttal at the ready.

We stopped at an intersection. Case tapped my shoulder and gestured for me to follow him. He took off down a lone street with more empty lots than buildings. I wasn't sure what we were going to find once we arrived, but I knew there was no easy way to get Luce back.

We weren't getting out of town unseen.

At the end of the street, the station loomed in the distance. The nondescript one-story building had a tall fence running around it, the main city wall, made of thick concrete, just beyond. It was obviously the station, because it was the only thing around with any lights on.

"They don't skimp on battery power around here," I commented. "It's bright enough to light up the entire block."

"It looks like they're expecting something," Case said. "The last time I was here, it was mostly dark, only a few lights on."

That didn't bode well for us. Since the Port Station guards were easily bribed, it was unsurprising that they'd be on the lookout for me. If Lockland or Case could get to them, so could Tandor's men.

"Where do you think they put her?" I asked. "The fence doesn't look too tall. If we can get close to it, I can stand on your shoulders and check out the interior."

"That might work," Case said. "If one of the guards tried to fly your craft, would they be successful?"

My lip curled in disgust. "Of course not."

"Would the entire craft blow?"

"No," I hedged. "Well, not at first." Risking my only means of transportation with a damaging explosion on a would-be thief's first attempt to steal her would be counterintuitive, especially since mistakes happened. "She won't start." I had a failsafe button I engaged with the toe of my boot each time I punched her on. It was seamlessly crafted below the dash and covered by a partition gap. My boot fit perfectly into the space. Tapping it was second nature. I wasn't going to share any of this with Case as we crept closer to the station, trying to figure out the best way in. "But if they try to start her more than five times, the sixth would spark a small kinetic bomb inside the engine," I said. "But it wouldn't kill anybody. It's placed to do specific damage I can fix." Making sure it was small was a priority, in case it blew up on its own, which could happen, even though kinetic bombs were pretty stable.

Case grunted. His favorite method of responding.

As we circled the building, I spotted something unusual and propelled Case behind a pile of debris twice as tall as we were.

"What?" he asked in a hushed tone.

"There's a small building tucked behind the main enclosure, outside the fence, and while I was watching, a light snapped on. The light is only visible along a thin horizontal line. There must be a crack between the wall of the building and the roof line."

"So?"

I tried not to let my impatience show. "Lockland said they had a mover drone. They used it to get Luce off the building. That kind of drone has to be twice the size of an average craft. It would need to be kept in a large enclosure, possibly a structure of its own. I'm just hypothesizing here, since we obviously won't know until we see it, but that annex building fits the bill. I think we should try there first."

Case looked pensive. "You're right, the mover drone might be parked there, but I'd think they'd want your craft where they could monitor it, which would be *inside* the main gates."

I nodded. "Could be. Or that's where the mechanics are, and they're trying to get her started. Who knows how many guards were bribed? It would garner less attention if they kept her outside the main gates." I settled my hands on my hips. "Why are we even debating this? All we have to do is go look. If Luce's not there, we figure out how to breach the interior."

A loud grating noise sounded, followed by props in the distance.

Both Case and I scanned the sky. The noise had come from the main gate, which sounded like it was in the process of being rolled back, making loud scraping sounds as it went. The propellers were getting closer.

"Someone's on their way in," Case said.

"Looks that way," I agreed. "This is our only chance. We're not getting another one."

Ducking down, we both ran, heading in an arc around the station. The place was lit up, but the darkened perimeter would keep us cloaked, better than if the lights had been off. The brightness from within would make it difficult to detect anything in the darkness beyond.

As we got closer, dead trees began to dot the area, giving us places to take cover if need be. "Let's hope the guards are distracted by the incoming visitors," I whispered.

"It's unusual for the guard station to open this late at night," he said.

"Honestly, you'd think this place would be crawling with guards on foot trying to protect the residents, especially after the shootout we had a few days ago."

"The guards don't seem to be worried."

That meant something.

"When you first followed Tandor up here from the South a few months ago, did he stop in Port Station?" We crouched behind a large tree trunk. We were halfway to the annex, but it was in our best interests to make sure we weren't seen.

"He was here for a few weeks. I didn't stay in Port Station because I knew his end goal. I figured this was just cover until he found an adequate place of operations in the city, which he did."

Tandor had been here far too long before I got wind of it, which was wholly unacceptable. If Tandor had stopped in Port Station first, not a single speck of gossip had trickled down to me or my crew, which was odd. People talked, especially when there were murmurings of a government takeover. Lockland had connections here as well. Ones he paid well. Someone should've said something. "How could Tandor wield so much influence in such a short amount of time?"

"Fear."

I shook my head. He had hardly been a leader who'd sparked fear in the hearts of anyone—just the opposite. He'd been whiny and wholly unimpressive. "He came off as weak to me. It's astounding he was able to accomplish anything at all."

"When people are scared, they react predictably."

"What were they scared of?"

"Being infected with Plush."

I thought back to the seeker, Cozzi, Dill, and Ned. They were all involved. Not only did I still have to find Ned, but I was determined to get more information out of Cozzi. The old guy and I went way back, and Case was right, he'd been fearful. The Cozzi I knew and loved would've fought back. They must've done more than threaten him. He must've witnessed something firsthand.

I focused my attention on the now clearly visible structure behind the station. The light was still on. The gap between the building's wall and the roof was less than a meter wide, not enough to fit through, but it would give us ample space to see what was going on. I'd have to stand on Case's shoulders, but it was doable. "How do you want to work this?" I asked. "If Luce is inside, we have to make a decision fast." The props were much louder now. The new craft would enter the guard area in less than two minutes.

"We make our way to the annex, I lift you up, and we go from there," Case said.

If Luce was inside, there was definitely a guard or two stationed there to watch her. We were going to have to take them out as quietly as possible. Once I had her up in the air, I was confident I could lose any threat. Her modified tech could fool even the most up-to-date radio frequency programs.

"Okay, let's go," I said as I ducked from behind the tree and began to run. I was certain the guards didn't think regular people would venture back here—or if they did, they had a death wish. Anyone caught would pay the price—including us.

We made it to the side of the annex right as the

craft entered the main area inside the fence. The props were exceptionally loud. There were only a few models with propellers that big. My guess was an X class. The X's were known for their fan dimensions. Their claim to fame was rock-solid stability even in heavy wind. Industrial companies favored them as working crafts.

Case barely stopped before he bent over. I vaulted onto his back, grabbing on to a tiny ledge that ran around the building to help support my weight. I needed to be hoisted up ten more centimeters. I tapped my foot on his shoulder.

He got the message. His breath was labored as he steadied his gloved hands under the soles of my boots and lifted me up. It worked.

Inside the structure, the room was wide open. The mover craft was there, along with two other crafts. Neither of which was Luce.

Four guards, dressed in standard uniforms of drab green, sat on chairs talking with what looked to be a mechanic, who stood wiping his dirty hands with a cloth. Once he was finished, he headed to a door on the other side of the building.

As he pulled it open, I caught a glimpse of Luce. Only the lower quadrant from behind, but I was positive it was my craft. I'd know her anywhere.

I was just about to jump down, when I heard one of the guards call to the retreating man, "You better get that thing started, Sabin. They're going to be here in a couple minutes. If it's not working, your head's on the cutting block, not mine."

"I'm close," Sabin replied. "Try to stall them for a few. It's rigged with a failsafe. I just haven't found it yet." He closed the door. I hoped that wasn't the only entrance into that stall. If it was, this was going to get messy fast.

We were breaking Luce out no matter what.

"Bullshit," I whispered as I jumped down. "He's not close to starting her." I landed on my feet and cocked my head toward the corner of the building, signaling that that was the way we had to go.

I led the way.

At the edge of the structure, I was relieved to see the main garage that housed the four guards was shuttered. The tall accordion door that could open to accommodate the mover drone was firmly closed. Without hesitating, I took off, running to the next corner.

Once there, I stopped and listened.

The only sound I could detect nearby was the mechanic clanking some tools around. I ducked my head out, glad to see this accordion door was open, light spilling into the night. Luce was in there, and I was about to get her back.

From somewhere inside the main guard area, loud voices erupted.

I pulled Case close, my mouth moving against his ear. "I only saw one mechanic. There are four guards in the other room. We take out the lone guy, try not to alert the other guards, commandeer my craft, and get the fuck out." Imagining it would be that easy was bordering on fiction, but I was still hopeful. Hope was the foundation of our world, after all. Without it, we might as well give the hell up.

Case nodded. The voices in the main area were getting louder. It was time to act. I darted around the corner, running a few steps before entering the stall with my weapons drawn. A guard—one I hadn't seen before—jumped up, but before I could fire, Case took the shot.

The guard's body began to shake uncontrollably.

Within moments, he collapsed onto the floor, jerking and convulsing, fluid streaming out of his eyes, ears, and nose.

Scratch that, those *were* his eyes.

They had liquefied.

"Jesus," I muttered as Case headed to the door that connected the rooms to lock it. My eyes landed on the mechanic, who, like myself, had been staring in stark horror at the guard leaking his insides all over the ground. He had his hands up, one still clutching the dirty rag. I kept my voice low. "If you don't want the same fate as that poor bastard, go sit in that chair." I gestured to a seat on his right. "Keep your arms up." I moved farther into the room, skirting my craft, as the mechanic did as I asked. I was happy to see Luce in one piece. Her hood was up, but all her parts were intact. "We're going to take this craft here and leave without any trouble. It's mine, so technically we're not stealing anything."

The mechanic said nothing as he sat, his face drawn.

I shut the hood as Case moved around to the other side, his gun aimed at the guy.

I harnessed my taser, since Case's magnetic pulse gun was way scarier, and reached into my pocket. I withdrew a carbon cube and held it between my fingers. "You're going to hold on to this," I told the mechanic, "and if you don't do as I say, it explodes. Understood?"

The mechanic recoiled as I approached. I held it out, but he refused to open his hand.

"If you don't take this in the next two seconds, I'm shoving it into your ear, and I'm fairly certain you won't be able to get it out before it explodes." The door behind us rattled as the guards on the other side tried to get through. "And you'll wish you went like that"—I nodded my head toward the dead guy on the floor—"because it would be much, much faster." Reluctantly, the mechanic held out his hand, and I dropped the cube into it. I reached into my vest for effect and said, "I just activated it. If you keep it stabilized, it will disengage in ten minutes. Understood?"

The guy nodded, looking a little queasy.

Case was already in the passenger seat of Luce.

I walked to the pilot's side and jumped in. In front of us, the guard room door was one shot away from being obliterated. Behind us, a loud shout sounded as a group of people rounded the fence sixty meters away.

We were about to be surrounded on both sides.

"Get out of here!" Case yelled.

"Working on it." I slammed the door, while simultaneously thrusting my Gem into Case's hand. "Use this. It'll do more long-range damage than your pulse. But use it with the window down." I started her up, toe where it should be, while engaging the left lever. Luce shot backward, right as the door in front of us burst open. The guards rushed out with their weapons drawn.

Twisting one hundred and eighty degrees, I hit the rarely needed hydro-boost. As Luce rocketed away, I continued her rotation as she expelled a long stream of hydrogen behind her. Everyone in the prop wash would be blown backward, including those assholes coming around the corner. And I'd managed to do it before anyone got in a debilitating shot.

I chuckled as I sped out of the area, wishing I could see the mechanic's face when he realized he'd been holding nothing more than a fuel cell.

Chapter 12

"That gun of yours is completely disgusting," I said as we sped toward the city. I wasn't ready to go back to the barracks yet. I wanted to try to get a hold of my crew first, and to do that, being closer was necessary. It'd been too long since I'd heard from anyone, and the gut worry had morphed into entire-body anxiety. I was crackling with it. Though, that could be from the heady dose of adrenaline I'd just received from Luce's awesome jailbreak.

"It's no different than blowing a hole through someone," he argued.

"You're right in theory," I agreed. "But you liquefied that guy. His eyeballs were leaking out of his face, and his brain was oozing out of his ears. Nobody wants to go like that. It's gross."

"Dead is dead."

"People have been known to survive a laser blast to

the foot, but nobody lives if one of those pellets gets into their bloodstream."

"That's true."

I spotted the city skyline in the distance. "We'll have to get your craft later." I'd boosted us out of there and given us a good lead. Circling back for Seven was impossible. Case had parked her well enough away and camouflaged her as best he could. As long as the guards didn't find her, it should be fine.

"What about the quantum drive?" he asked. "Is it still here?"

"I haven't checked yet," I answered. "But if you turn your head, I'll look." I wasn't going to give away my hiding spot.

While Case did as I asked, I popped open the compartment directly above my right knee. It had been built seamlessly into the molding.

With great relief, the small chip fell into my outstretched palm.

I exhaled.

Not finding it here would've been devastating on a number of levels. Recovering the quantum drive had now propelled us ahead of the game. We had access to something that Hutch likely needed to implement his dastardly plans. It'd been important to Tandor—so important he died for it. He'd called the drive "the key."

The key to what was the mystery.

But hopefully not for long.

"Well?" Case asked, his face still angled toward the passenger window.

I tucked the small chip into a vest pocket. The pico was still safely nestled against my abdomen. It was so small I barely knew it was there. "I have it."

In that moment, I realized I'd given Case my Gem.

I tensed. If Case planned to double-cross me to get the quantum drive, now would be a good time to make his move.

With a look of disdain, and without being asked, Case spun the barrel of my Gem around and handed it to me butt first. It was dark, so I couldn't see his expression, but I could picture it. It was a combination of *I told you so* and *this is getting old.*

I took the gun and holstered it at my waist, arching my lower half off the seat to get it secured. "You can't blame me for thinking you're going to turn on me. You've done it a few times already. Practice makes perfect."

He sighed. It was a low, quiet sound. "Everything I've done so far was to protect myself. Nothing more."

"And exact revenge," I said. He couldn't forget about his nonbiological sister. She was the reason he'd come to the city in the first place. She killed his nephew in cold blood, under Tandor's orders, and he'd come to avenge the boy. It was a fairly noble reason, if he hadn't used me in the process.

"Yes."

I leaned forward in my seat. Morning would be upon us in less than an hour, judging by the sky. It was hard to notice the subtle brightening, as it never got very light, but having lived here for the last twenty-seven years, and making it my business to know, I was pretty good at judging the time between day and night.

The city was outlined in stark contrast to everything around it, broken and battered, the buildings arrayed on the horizon like a line of chipped teeth, angular and sharp, in danger of causing harm if you weren't careful. The clouds were misting less than a full drizzle. It was unusual for the rain to be this light, but I wasn't complaining.

Instead of going straight into the city, my plan was to land just outside, by our rarely used east entrance. Not so rare, since I'd used it the other day with Case, but obsolete enough. There was no reason to go in if my crew wasn't around. If I failed to make contact, finding them would be my new number-one problem to solve.

Dropping altitude, I maneuvered closer, nudging the craft east. Case and I rode in silence. My brain whirled with the implications of Tandor's men in charge of Port Station. If they'd taken over that area—and no gossip had leaked—something major was happening or about to happen. It was hard to believe the threat of Plush was enough to keep the masses silent, but being forced to become a seeker would carry some terrifying consequences.

Logically, it had to be more than that. We just had to figure out what the threat was. I was confident the quantum drive would hold some answers.

There was no use blindfolding Case this time. We

were beyond that. If there was another betrayal, someone's life would end.

Finally reaching our destination, I punched Luce's landing gear, setting her down thirty meters outside the entrance behind a copse of dead, gnarled trees. I kept her running as I pulled out a tech phone. "Jerry, it's Ella." I prayed that Lockland would pick up. I needed something, some nugget of information that told me they were okay.

Nothing.

I tried again. "Jerry, come in. Hoping to meet for breakfast." I nudged Case with my arm, gesturing to the compartment in front of him. He obliged, opening it. I tried again, depressing the button on the side. "Johnny, are you there?" I reached in and plucked out the static wand I kept in there, flicking a switch on the side to turn it on as I powered down my dashboard, cutting off all radio transmissions Luce produced herself.

The tip of the wand glowed a warm yellow, indicating it was working. It would blink if it picked up any signaling radio waves. I swiped the stick around the dash. When it got close to my tech phone, it began to blink.

I tucked the phone in a vest pocket and stuck the wand down by my feet.

"If they put a tracker on Luce, it's likely in the battery compartment," Case said.

I nodded, but refrained from commenting *duh*, as I took the phone back out and set it to a new channel, one of our other private bandwidths. We had four. I depressed the button as I opened Luce's door, stepping out onto the wet, puddled ground. "It's Kate. Wondering if anyone's out there?"

While I waited for a response, I waved the wand around the craft, popping the battery compartment to give it a thorough sweep. It was clean. But as I rounded the back and swept up under the storage area, the light began to flicker.

Leaning over, I spotted the culprit.

I picked the tracker off the bottom, where it had been secured magnetically, and dropped it on the ground. It made a satisfying crack as I ground my heel into it.

If they hadn't placed a tracker on Luce, it would've been negligence on their part. The question was, had they placed more trackers that operated on other frequencies? Longwave frequency was the only thing that could filter through our iron-heavy air reliably. But shortwave high frequency in compact bursts could work, although the connection was always spotty and unreliable.

I clicked the button on the wand down a notch, and the light at the end of the stick glowed blue. Then I proceeded to search the craft again. Once I got close to the battery compartment, it began to flicker. I tucked my tech phone into a vest pocket as I hefted the lid back up.

Case joined me in front as I ran the static wand over the motor. I wasn't extremely familiar with high-frequency trackers, so I wasn't certain what to look for. I'd seen only a few before, and they came in all different shapes and sizes.

We both bent over as the wand located the monitor by blinking without ceasing. This one was bigger than the one I'd just crushed beneath my boot and a strange color—charcoal with an amber hue. I'd reached in to grab it when Case stilled my arm, his grip like a vise. "It looks rigged."

I glanced at him, surprised. "Have you used high-frequency trackers before?"

"Not myself, but I've seen more than a few of them. This one is bigger than it should be." Larger could mean it contained condensed hydrogen, like the nano-carbon cubes I used.

Once dislodged, it could blow.

"If we don't get rid of it, they track us. There's a possibility they have better high-frequency-monitoring tech than we do. I don't know that much about Port Station and what advances they've made in the last twenty years. That town is not good at sharing." I was going to make it my business to learn more once this was all finished.

"We're going to interrupt it. Do you have a jammer on you?"

"Of course." I reached into an internal pocket and pulled out a jammer. It was roughly the size of a fingernail and magnetic. I'd used this on Case's craft so it couldn't record our flight directions. Jammers interrupted radio signals, but as far as I knew, they didn't work on broadcast signals, only local ones within the craft itself. I handed it to him. "It won't stop that thing from transmitting a frequency that they're tuned in to."

He leaned over and stuck the jammer next to the tracker. "No, it won't, but it should alter the frequency just enough to make it almost impossible to track or detonate remotely. Add that to the inconsistency of high frequency, and we should be safe."

"Safe is a relative term." I didn't like knowing it was in there, because if it was also a hydro-bomb, it could go off on its own. "Bender will have to take a look at it once he gets back. He'll be able to get it out of there."

Speaking of Bender, where the hell were they?

My tech phone went off.

I scrambled to get it out of my vest. "Kate, it's Larry." Lockland's voice came through the speaker. "Found our quest. Entering the area."

They'd been out of range that long? The "area" was how we defined our communication zone.

There wasn't much out there. The government did have a few secret locations where they conducted interviews and such. My best guess was that Darby had been held in one of those spots. But I wasn't going to ask now, nor was Lockland going to divulge anything like that over the airwaves.

"Sounds good. I'll be ready in three," I said. "I'm planning on bringing Rennie and a few presents for Don's birthday." I was letting them know that I'd gotten Luce and the quantum drive back and that I would bring Daze with me in three hours. The real surprise would be the pico. "I'll hit you when I'm close."

"Excellent. See you then." He signed off, and the phone went dark. No static indicated he'd turned it off on his end. I wasn't sure what had happened, but the relief I felt knowing they were okay was immense. They had Darby, and they would've mentioned Claire if there were any issues, so my family was safe.

At least for the time being.

They had no idea that my residence had been blown up, or that it was possible Tandor's men had taken over Port Station and were infecting people with Plush. There would be a lot to sort out in a few hours.

It was time to head back to the barracks and pick up Daze. I hoped the kid knew what he was talking about when it came to the pico.

Walking around the craft to the pilot's side, I got in. Once Case was secured, I took off, spinning Luce around so she was heading toward the sea. "When we get back, I want you to get rid of all your voice amplifiers and whatever else you have lying around the bunker until Daze's done with his treatments. No more breaches of trust."

Case turned toward me, giving me a rare grin. "If I do, does that mean you're going to start trusting me?"

"Hell, no."

Chapter 13

The pico was propped open on the tech table in front of Daze. I sat next to him, Case stood behind. The kid tapped a bunch of buttons, but nothing happened. He fidgeted in his seat, his face drawn. "The battery is dead," he said. "It won't turn on."

"Are you sure?" I reached over and pressed what looked to be the power key, which was big and green. I gave it a few taps, including holding it down. He was right, it was dead. The helium batteries designed for these things were supposed to last for years. As far as I knew, they weren't replaceable, as they were integrated into the unit.

Pre-dark days, technology had changed at a rapid rate. In order to keep up with the next new thing, you didn't replace batteries, you bought the next superfast computer. Data readers came in all shapes and sizes and had been an everyday necessity for humans. Contrary to the pico sitting in front of us, which was priceless because we couldn't go out and get another one, a computer back in the day had cost less than a subscription to your favorite media channel.

The quantum drive lay forlorn on the table, containing a massive amount of information ripe for the taking, but we couldn't get to it because of a dead battery.

"Does this computer have charging capabilities? If the battery is just dead, and not spent, it should work if we can get power to it." Case leaned forward, bracing his hands on the back of the couch. "Most computers before the dark days had integrated charging, especially the quality ones. I would think a pico, which was dedicated to reading a quantum drive, would have one. Some of them even had solar capabilities, but I don't see any of the telltale squares molded into the top."

Daze shrugged. "I don't know. All I ever did was play around on it."

I picked up the computer and turned it over in my hands. It was light and easy to handle. "What am I looking for? There are slots on the sides, but nothing looks like it connects to a power source."

"Hand it to me," Case said.

I gave it to him, growling, "If anything happens to it, I can't be held responsible for my actions."

Case snorted as he flipped it over, running his fingers along the bottom. "Before the dark days, if you didn't have access to an open-air recharge system, you used a charging pad. They were integrated into furniture and counters, so they didn't take up excess space. By the end of the NewGen era, they only needed to be a few atoms thick to work."

"That's great," I said, glancing around, "but where are we going to get a NewGen era charging pad? I'm a salvager and I've never seen one."

"Like I said, they were mostly built into furniture." Case walked around the couch into the kitchen area. He set the pico down and began to run his hands over the countertop.

I joined him. "Would one of these charging surfaces actually be obvious to the touch?"

"Not sure," Case said. "But I think the surface above the charger would feel a little different, possibly scuffed from wear. This was a working barracks. The soldiers in here would need to charge their tech."

Both of our hands swept the surface, but I didn't feel anything different.

An excited squeal erupted behind us. Daze had knelt next to the tech table, his arms spread wide over the surface. "I think I found a couple places. One of them has a bunch of marks on it." His head was tilted almost horizontal to the thing.

We walked over, Case bending over to investigate. "You might be right."

"Super," I said. "But the tech table isn't operational, is it?"

"It could be. I never bothered to try to turn it on." Case paced to the wall by the entrance that held a bunch of switches. He began to flip them. A couple lights blinked on in one corner. One initiated a fan somewhere in the back. But the tech table stayed dark.

Undeterred, he headed to a patch of wall where a shelving unit sat, stacked with obsolete cooking utensils and a bunch of random boxes. He shouldered the thing out of the way with a loud grating sound, the items bouncing around.

The uncovered wall revealed another row of switches.

One by one, Case flipped them on. When he hit the very last one, the tech table sprang to life.

Daze and I both clapped our hands. I couldn't help it. It was such a relief. Blue and red lights flickered as some welcoming words flashed across the screen. This table would've been used to make military plans. Maps and essential information would've been hardwired into its memory, all paired with adaptive 3-D hologram capability. The images would've been displayed above the table. It'd probably been a gathering place in the barracks.

Case set the pico on the scuffed area Daze had found. "I'm not sure how long it will take."

"I'll stay here and wait until it powers on." Daze's voice was filled with excitement as he plunked down, crossing his arms on the table, his chin resting on top, his eyes focused on the pico like a pair of amber lasers. I had no doubt he'd stay like that for hours if need be. Or until something else caught his attention.

"Have you been in the medi-pod lately?" I asked. "We're taking off as soon as that thing powers up, so now's the time."

A frown formed as he claimed, "I feel better. I don't need that thing anymore. Everything is fixed. See?" He moved his arm up and down and rapped his knuckles on his chest.

"Sorry, kid," I said, my hand dipping down to tousle his hair. "I understand the allure of waiting for the pico to power on, but if you don't use the medi-pod until the treatment's done, you won't feel better anymore. Your vitamin D levels were extremely low, and your broken bones might feel pain-free now, but they're not fully healed. They could easily break again. Come on, let's go. When you're done, the pico will be ready, and I promise we'll wait until you're back to turn it on."

Reluctantly—like the kid had iron pellets stuffed in his pockets—he stood and shuffled toward the back of the barracks. I placed my hand on his shoulder as we walked. "After we figure out what's on the quantum drive, we're heading to Bender's to fill everyone in. They're going to be pumped to hear what we find."

"Oh," he said glumly.

I picked up on his despondent tone. "What's wrong?"

"They don't like me anymore. I lied to everyone."

I opened the lid, and he crawled inside. Once he was situated, I said, "They like you just fine. I gave them your apology, and you can back it up when we get there. You had to do what you had to do to survive. That's the name of the game. In the end, you tried to sacrifice yourself to save us. That's huge." He looked unsure, so I added, "Bender has a gift for you."

His face brightened. "What?"

"I can't tell you, but it starts with a W."

"Is it a weapon?" His voice was hopeful. "I bet it's a weapon."

"I'm not about to ruin the surprise. Bender would kill me." I lowered the lid. "Stay in here until it beeps. No excuses."

"Fine," he grumbled.

I made sure the display blinked with the patient number he'd been assigned with his diagnosis, and then I pressed the button labeled *Heal.* The outer shell of the pod began to spin. Once I was satisfied it was working, I made my way back to Case, who sat in front of the pico. I took a seat across from him. "Has it powered on yet?"

His helmet was off, his brow drawn. "No."

"You know, Case,"—I settled back on the couch, crossing my legs—"I'm not sure how we move on from here. I still don't trust you. Letting you see what's on the quantum drive"—I nodded toward the pico, which was hopefully charging, getting ready to unleash its secrets—"puts me in a precarious position with my friends. I realize you helped me get the computer and break Luce out of Port Station. You gave me back my Gem and found a way to jam the tracker. But that doesn't make you an ally. There could be some very sensitive things on that drive, and if you happen to be working for the other side, the advantage I just gained by retrieving that prize is gone."

His gray eyes fastened on mine. He sat silent for a while before responding. "I'm not used to working as a team."

I waited for more, but none came. "So? And I care about that why?"

He ran both his hands through his hair, straightening up. "What's it going to take for you to trust me? Not blind trust, but the beginning of something we can work with?" Case had already admitted that he wasn't going back to where he'd come from. That meant he was going to be around awhile—if not indefinitely. He was a thorn that was going to continue to prick me whether I liked it or not.

Instead of answering, I glanced around the large space we occupied. The barracks was a pretty sweet setup, and he hadn't complained once about letting us use it. The supplies in here would feed all of us for a few years, no problem. Having one of my residences blown to bits was a reminder that I was going to have to salvage hard for more resources, including ways to gather power.

I was momentarily distracted.

Uncrossing my legs, I stood, turning in a full circle, realizing I hadn't seen a main power supply to this place since I'd been here. "Where are the batteries located?" My voice came out sounding confused, which was fairly accurate. I had my residences rigged with wires running from solar panels to battery packs. It was all very conspicuous. "Where does the energy come from to work the lights and stuff?"

Case stood, saying nothing, and began to head toward the back of the room.

I followed.

We passed the medi-pod, which whirred quietly, doing whatever it did to make someone well again. At the end, there were two doors—one led to a waste room, and the other I hadn't investigated before. Case opened the second door and reached in to turn on a light. I leaned in behind him, glancing over his shoulder, and my breath caught in my throat.

The entire room was filled with batteries.

Not small batteries, like the kinds I'd clustered in packs and mounted on my wall. These were big half-a-meter-square helium batteries. The kind only the government had access to, even before the dark days. A single one was rumored to last five years from one full charge. These kinds of batteries had been completely salvaged in the first few years after the meteor hit. I'd never found even a single one in all my years searching, which was saying something.

This room held hundreds.

"What?" My face probably mirrored the incredulousness I felt.

He entered, and I trailed behind. As far as I was concerned, these were hunks of solid gold. Stacks upon stacks of living, breathing vitality. If anyone—let alone the government—ever found out they were here, we'd be dunked in a vat of acid and questioned later.

"Showing you this has to count for something, right?" His voice held humor. His stubble was beginning to grow back. From this close, I could see it was a shade or two darker than the hair on his head.

"Possibly. Better would be letting me take some."

"Be my guest."

I gave him a look, a cross between an eye roll and an eyebrow waggle. "You'd just give me these? Like it didn't matter? You know as well as I do what these batteries mean—they mean life. They mean wealth. They mean resources. And death, if the wrong people find out—hell, if *anyone* found out. These have murder written all over them." I made a sweeping arm gesture. "Almost every human left in the world would kill for these."

He seemed unfazed. "I only need enough to run this place."

"How do they stay charged?" I wandered over to one, my fingers tracing the hard contours. It was warm. "It's been over sixty years since disaster struck, and you said the sand had eroded only enough for the barracks to be spotted ten years ago. That means they went without charge for fifty years. No battery lasts that long, not even helium technology."

He moved a stack, uncovering a small shuttered opening situated halfway up the wall. Grabbing on to a knob, he yanked the façade down. Inside was filled with wires.

Solar.

I'd never seen the roof of the barracks. We'd always arrived and departed over the sea. "Are the panels visible from the air?" I asked.

"Semi," he answered, closing the space up. "You'd have to know what you were looking for. They're military-grade glass, like a megascraper window, but stronger, with more output. When I first found this place, some were too scratched to salvage, but luckily there were enough to power this entire room. Back when this place was fully operational, there were likely other spaces just like this, but they've been destroyed, likely caved in."

"How long did it take for the batteries to become optimal?"

"Six days."

I whistled. That was impressive. We made our way out, Case shutting the door behind us. We had to face facts—neither was going to leave the other alone with that pico.

Case veered toward the cooling unit, and I continued to the tech table. "Do you want something to eat?" he asked. "It seems Daze took your words to comb this place to heart." I glanced over to see the piles of dried-food packets stacked around the cooling unit. Case picked up a package. "This one says it's meatloaf flavored." He squinted at the lettering. "Do you know what that is?"

I shook my head. "Nope. But whatever is fine."

He heated some water and made two bags, walked over, and handed one to me. "If you don't like it, there's more to choose from." He gestured idly toward the countertop.

I took a bite. "Wasting food is not my thing," I said between scoops. "So unless it tastes like excrement, which it doesn't, I'm fine." We ate in silence for a few minutes. Once I was done, I set the bag on the table. I tried to run my hands through my hair, but my fingers couldn't get through it. I badly needed a shower, but it was going to have to wait. I took a deep breath. "Okay, Case. We have an hour and a half before we head out. I want to hear your story. Leave nothing out, and don't lie to me. After you're done, I'll tell you if it's enough."

He raised his eyebrows. "Enough what?"

"For me to trust you."

Chapter 14

For a moment, it didn't seem like Case was going to answer my request for his backstory. He got up and paced, ending up against a pillar near the cooling unit. He braced his shoulder against the painted metal column and started, "My parents were part of a small tribe in the South, in what used to be called South Carolina. We call them tribes because that's what they are. Not cities, not towns—but small human collectives trying their damnedest to stay alive. Every waking hour is a fight to stay fed and keep breathing. My parents would've come to the city to try to better their lives, but they had no resources or means—no craft, no transportation of any kind—so they stayed." This wasn't going to be an uplifting tale, but then, most of ours weren't. "The eastern shoreline of the United States, as you know, was one of the only places to survive the meteor hits. It was far enough away from all three impacts, even though it'd been battered by the aftermath of hurricanes and tsunamis. My ancestors did us a disservice by believing they could make these small communities work, that they had any lasting sustainability. They didn't. In reality, they dug themselves into a deep hole they couldn't get out of. It was only a matter of time before all the resources were depleted and nothing was left. By the time my parents had me, the tribe was less than one hundred strong, and the conditions were abysmal." He pushed off the pillar, walked over to the cooling unit, and took out water. After he poured himself a cup, he took a long drink. His eyes were full of fatigue, his face slack.

Filling in the gap of his long pause, I said, "I've heard tales over the years about these kinds of communities, none of it good." The stories are full of hardship, sorrow, and death. "I've never understood how people could live with less than we have here, because life here sucks."

He nodded, setting the cup down and coming to sit across from me. "There had been immediate salvaging along the coast directly after the meteor. The community where I grew up had amassed what they thought was enough to keep them going for many years—and it had—but as the years turned into decades, the stocks ran low. Then The Water Initiative began. Recruiters from the city came to the Southern communities in droves, under the guise of bringing aid, only to convince those with the most resources among us to go along with them. Overnight, the last of the vital necessities were gone, carried away by the assholes who decided to join the quest for a better life at the cost of all of ours."

There was no way to know if the planned Flotilla—a massive city on water—had thrived, or if the hundreds of boats laden with supplies had been taken to their watery graves at the mercy of the fierce, roiling sea.

I clasped my hands in front of me, leaning forward, my elbows resting on my thighs. "The Water Initiative harmed us all in irreparable ways," I said. "In fact, at the rate we're going, I'd give it another ten years before we're all extinct. I don't know what they were thinking, but obviously only about themselves."

Case's eyes took on a faraway look as they focused somewhere behind my shoulder. "I was born the year the Flotilla set sail. Both my parents died four years later, within six months of each other. The medic in charge of the tribe had taken all the inoculations with him." Case met my gaze, his gray eyes flashing in anger. "After that, my life was a living hell. An older couple sustained me for three years, and even though they meant well, I was nothing more than their prisoner. They never allowed me to go outside because they were so fearful of what might happen, so they kept me locked in a small room." His voice took on a wistful note. "But they fed me, often giving me more than they had themselves, and the room had a sleeping pod, which provided me with some entertainment and a daily dose of UV. After the old man died, I broke out. I was seven years old. I wandered the streets for close to a year." He shook his head. "It's a mystery I survived at all. There were weeks I went without food. A new family who were passing through, one outside the tribe, offered to take me in if I was willing to work. I was one of their many sustainees. I was happy to do hard labor. Anything for a home."

"The same family who took in your sister?"

"Yes. I met Carmen a few months before that on the street. She was two years older than me. The work was hard, but it paid off in the end, because it made me strong and capable. The family was convinced we could all save ourselves if we just tried hard enough." Sorrow seeped into his voice. "They were part of a tribe who considered themselves Sun Optimists. If they did the higher power's bidding, the sun would grace us once again. The work they deemed holy was digging underground shelters. Day and night, that's all we did. It was backbreaking, but we always had a place to lay our heads out of the rain. The saving grace was that they had a large 3-D bio-printing machine with enough slurry to keep it running, so we always had enough food."

Slurry was a basic atomic mixture that was added to the bio-printers to make food. In order to create it, you needed access to a macro-centrifuge, which separated organic material by density, filtering out the unneeded waste. The end result looked exactly like it sounded— like a pile of sludgy stuff you poured into your bio-printer. The results were dry, crumbly protein cakes, with little variation.

"I left a day before my sixteenth birthday."

"Then what?" I asked. There were a lot of years from sixteen until now.

He was quiet. I let him take his time. His gaze finally met mine. "Militia members recruited me. I was tall for my age, and because of the years of hard work, I was what they referred to as able-bodied." The corners of his eyes compressed. "They fed me lines about being able to save the world. That I would be one of the few who could keep our community safe. I would be its protectorate. I bought it, so I agreed to go with them." He shrugged. Then he bowed his head. "They were all lies."

"Were they part of a child-slavery ring? Sixteen is a young recruit."

He ran a hand over his face, lingering on the stubble coating his chin. "Yep. They took glee in exploiting children." He stood, making his way around the couch. "If my life had been wretched before, it was infinitely worse. The abuse was…unbearable."

My heart gave a single clinch. I'd been there before. I'd lived that life.

His voice was hollow as he continued, his back to me. "The only redeeming thing was they taught me to fight. Both physically and mentally."

I closed my eyes as his pain echoed inside my soul. "How many years?" I could barely get the question out.

"Eight."

Eight horrifying years at the hands of abusers. "How did you escape?"

He turned around, his hands clasped behind his back. "A man happened into our community. The abusers—

posing as militia—protected five different tribes. It was clear this man had been trained—and trained well. He'd been militia someplace else. He was big, tough, with silver hair and a scar running along his jawline. He asked for entry into the group, and it was granted. He assimilated seamlessly and quickly moved up the ranks. Our leaders fell all over themselves trying to impress him, coaxing him into giving them his secrets." Case's eyes flicked over mine. Life had been hard for him. "I refused to give him the time of day, nor my loyalty. And for some reason—likely because of my ambivalence—he singled me out. He goaded me day and night, trying to get me to react like the others. It never worked." Case dropped his arms and came back to the couch, sitting, his face resigned. "Two days after my twenty-fourth birthday, he shook me awake in the dead of night." He bowed his head. "He'd killed them all. All my tormentors were gone, the entire militia wiped out. He'd wasted forty-six men without a sound. He told me to get dressed, so I did. We gathered up supplies, got into his craft—mine now—and went to a place similar to this one." He shrugged, sitting back, glancing around the barracks. "He made it his mission to train me. I never asked why." Case met my questioning glance. "You don't ask an angel why they choose to intervene, you just accept it. We moved from place to place. He always knew where to go, where to get more supplies. I suspected he was part of a larger network, but I never found out what it was. He was someone who would never betray a trust. He brought me here for the first time two years ago. We worked hard to uncover and reclaim it from the sand. He died six months ago. I buried him up on the dunes." Case walked over to the cooling unit. "During my time with him, I'd reacquainted myself with my old Sun Optimist sustainer family and kept in touch. The parents had died, but the children remained close. After Dixon, the man who trained me, passed away, I headed back South. My arrival happened to coincide with Tandor's. His crew had gone from tribe to tribe recruiting members, a familiar tactic, just like The Water Initiative." He opened up the cooler and took out some water. "Two weeks later, Carmen killed her child, and everything Dixon had instilled in me came to the forefront. I followed Tandor and his men up here, and you know the rest." He poured himself another glass, his gaze falling to the counter in front of him.

He was done.

There was still immense mystery shrouding this man, but it was a start. He'd laid the groundwork, like I'd asked, providing a seed of trust to be planted.

Assuming the story wasn't complete bullshit.

I nodded as I stood. "Thanks for sharing that with me. I appreciate it. I know the past is hard for most of us to dig up, let alone explain to a stranger."

He set the cup down and relaxed against the counter, bracing both his hands around the rim. Outwardly, he conveyed his ease, but I noted the tenseness of his shoulders and the stiff angle of his neck. "Did I pass your test?"

I stood. "It wasn't a test." The medi-pod timer went off. I was thankful for the distraction. "And, yes," I called over my shoulder, heading toward Daze, "if the story is truthful, it'll go a long way toward establishing the start of something."

What, I wasn't exactly sure. But I was glad he'd told me.

"It's real." His voice was coated in emotion, surprising me. "Even though I'd give every coin I've ever earned to change it."

"It's working," Daze exclaimed excitedly. "Look, the screen is blinking!" It'd taken less than an hour to charge, but it seemed the pico had miraculously been brought back to life.

"I see," I said. "Do you remember how to get into the files?"

"I think so." He tapped a few buttons. "This computer helped me learn to read." His chest puffed. "My dad was real smart. He even worked for the government when he was younger."

"Is that so?" I asked. "What did he do?"

Daze's brows furrowed. "I don't know. My mom never answered me when I asked. But I think he worked with numbers. There were a lot of numbers on this computer. And lots of files about AI and LiveBots. It's really cool. I can show you later if you want."

"That's great, but first we need it to read this." I picked up the quantum drive, carefully holding it by an edge. "Where do you insert it?" There were a number of slots on the side, but they all looked the same to me, and none of them looked like the drive would fit inside.

"That doesn't go anywhere regular," Daze said in a tone like I should know. "The quantum drive is special. It goes in its own place." He plucked the chip out of my hand while tapping something onto the screen with the other. Very slowly, a section of the computer broke away, rising like a mini hydro-lift. "It works!" Daze chirped as he carefully placed the quantum drive into the slot and pushed the drive down.

It slid easily, clicking into place, like it'd been waiting for the chance to merge with the supercomputer.

I held my breath.

There was too much on the line.

Almost immediately, rows and rows of text popped onto the screen, scrolling so fast none of us could keep up. We all leaned in closer. I squinted because the font was tiny and hard to read.

After a moment, I realized it wasn't standard text. It was numbers. Lots and lots of complex equations flying by, a page a second.

After a full minute, the data stopped scrolling. The cursor blinked on the bottom right, indicating the screen had stopped populating.

I met Case's confused expression. I was certain it mirrored my own. "Are those what I think they are?" I asked. "Did you see all the graphics?" Among the icons I saw flashing across the screen, mostly in the upper left corner, were those of Bliss Corp, SensiTouch, and the standard government seal, which consisted of a square blue background, a white circle with sixty-three red stars inside, and a red, white, and blue ribbon running through it.

Case answered, "Those were formulas."

I exhaled as my mind raced. "That stuff at the beginning had 'Top Secret' seals attached." I sat back. "How in the world did someone like Tandor get this information?" According to what we'd just seen and based on the companies involved, it seemed the government might've been aware of—or even been involved with—procuring a cure for Plush addiction. But I wasn't a mathematician or an engineer, so I didn't know for sure.

"I have no idea how a guy from a small tribe in the South would have access to something like this," Case answered. "When I asked around, I couldn't find any background on him. Nobody was willing to talk."

I stared at the screen. "This could change everything."

"What? What's going to change?" Daze asked.

I traced my finger across two logos at the top of the screen. "Do you see these names? Bliss Corp and SensiTouch? What's on this drive came from these companies. They worked together on enhancing Plush, after Bliss Corp initially put out the drug. Then, whatever they did to tweak the formula, it went bad, and people started reacting, and they became the seekers we see today. They were both trillion-dollar companies with lots and lots of power."

"Yeah." He nodded. "So?"

"Because the government was clearly involved, and it was top secret, this might be data for a cure. It would've been a priority for the government to find something to help infected people and hold these companies accountable." I stood. "But, honestly, Darby is the only one who can make sense of all this. The first thing we have to do is get this information to him."

Case was already headed toward the door. "Let's go."

Chapter 15

I piloted Luce in silence. We were on the way to drop Case off to retrieve Seven. The three of us had left the barracks shortly after discovering what was on the quantum drive.

Case sat in the passenger seat, Daze in the back.

My backseat had taken a hit, as I'd been forced to dump a bunch of stuff and leave it at the barracks so the kid would fit. Backseats in most crafts were cramped, and mine was no exception. But my penchant for storing stuff had made it impossible for anyone to squeeze in—even if they had the body size and type of an eight-year-old.

I hadn't handled the task in a completely adultlike fashion. There'd been grumbling and complaining, some swearing, but it hadn't killed me, so that was a bonus.

Daze, who was normally chatty, was quiet.

It was fine by me, as I was anxious to talk to my

crew, and we were running late. I'd told them three hours, but it was going to be more like four, and we weren't close enough to the city for me to check in yet.

"Set her down in a kilometer," Case said.

His request surprised me, and I directed my brain back on task. "We're too far out. It'll take you all day to walk in."

He shook his head. "It's too risky to fly any closer. If the guards are smart, they'll be monitoring the skies."

"I know. That's why I'm flying low." The bottom of Luce was almost scraping the treetops, I was so low.

"Set her down. I'll walk."

I shrugged. "Okay, whatever you want." Who was I to argue? It didn't matter to me where he got out. I found the next patch of open ground and landed, keeping her running while Case exited.

We'd agreed to part ways for the time being.

I'd take Daze back for treatment at the barracks sometime tomorrow. Case said he'd be there, but I could open the barracks myself if I needed to. There was nothing more to say. He gave me a three-finger salute and loped off in search of his craft. If she wasn't where we'd left her, he'd have to figure it out.

I lofted us back into the sky as Daze climbed into the front seat, his arms immediately punching through the harness straps. Smart man. "What are Bender and Lockland going to think about what's on the quantum drive?" he asked once he was situated. His voice held a fair amount of trepidation. I knew he was worried to see them again.

"They're going to think it's a pretty big deal," I said. "Darby is going to be crazy excited." I hoped to hell Darby was still with them. "He's going to know how to read all those complex formulas and numbers, and best of all, he'll be able to do something about it."

"Where are we going to go after I'm done using the medi-pod?" Daze asked, his tone soft and measured. He was worried about something.

"I'm not sure," I answered, keeping my voice light. Well, as light as it got, anyway. "That depends on what's happening in the city. We don't know if Darby spilled any information about my residence in the canals to the bad guys or the government. If he didn't, once we take care of the rest of Tandor's men, we can head to there. If not, I'm going to have to hunt for a new place to live." The scope of setting up a brand-new residence made my head hurt. The amount of effort and goods it took to make a place habitable was staggering. "We can use my unit in Government Square until we figure it out. It'll be a tight fit, but we can make it work." I gave him a look. "You're not nervous, are you?"

"No," he replied quickly. The kid's face was so full of relief it was almost comical. I wondered what was going through that brain of his.

"You know, Daze, you're not getting rid of me that easily. But if you want, I can talk to Case. I'm sure he'd be okay if you stayed in the barracks with him for a while. That is, until I set up a new, suitable unit." I watched his reaction carefully.

"No." His tone was rushed. "I don't want to do that. At least…not if you're not going to be there. I like it there. It's safe. But I don't want to…" He fidgeted with his hands.

I let him off the hook. "No problem. Together it is. We'll figure it out." I changed the subject. "You know, after we deal with all the stuff with Plush, and everything else, maybe we should take a vacation." I was only half joking. Nobody around here took a vacation. It was unheard of. But a scouting mission was not.

If I'd learned anything from Case, it was that the world was bigger than inside the city limits, the gorge, and Port Station. If the barracks existed—which I'd never thought possible—then what else was out there? The possibilities were vast. If we packed up enough supplies and had ample battery and hydrogen power, we could go out for a few weeks, no problem. It actually sounded fun.

A concept I wasn't well acquainted with.

The kid brightened instantly. "Really? I've never been anywhere. Well, except, you know, the places we've been together."

"It's pretty wild out there. We'd be taking our lives into our own hands. Are you sure you're up for something that huge?"

"Totally. I was born ready." He jutted his chin out as his thumbs expanded the straps of the harness in front of him, his chest puffing.

I tilted my head back and laughed. "Kid, you crack

me up." We were closing in on the city limits. I decided it would be best to go in stealthily, so I was heading to the entrance Daze and I had first used, on the west side. It was our most secure location. That way, Lockland could monitor our process if necessary. "I'm sure we'll have this all figured out in no time. Then we'll plan an expedition."

"Cool."

"Jerry, it's Ella." Static. "We're still waiting on that green light." Daze and I were in the craft, hovering in the old parking ramp, waiting for Lockland to turn the light green and open the wall.

We'd been waiting not so patiently for twenty minutes.

Something was wrong.

Crackling finally came over the line. "Change of plans." Lockland's voice was labored. Static. "Meet at six." Then nothing. He'd turned off his phone.

"Shit." I levered Luce into reverse, backing her speedily down the ramp, spinning her one hundred and eighty degrees, heading back the way we'd come.

"What does 'six' mean?" Daze asked.

"Remember that first night?" I said as I engaged the landing gear and set her down, the wall closing seamlessly behind us. "I parked in here because I was taking you to six, but then we ran into Darby and headed to my residence instead? Six is one of our safe houses, and it happens to be a few buildings over." It was one of our bigger places. It slept four.

"Are we going to have to walk over that beam again?" Daze's voice wavered at the end.

"Yep," I said as I powered the craft off. "But it's going to be easy, because everything we do is easy, remember?"

"What about seekers?"

"I'm sure Lockland has secured the place back up." When we'd been there last, we'd encountered seekers, and it'd been harrowing. We'd had to make a quick exit through the floor. I wasn't really sure Lockland had been here, but we were about to find out. It was unlikely Lockland would send us here if it hadn't been resecured. At least, I didn't think he would. It was possible he forgot what had gone down a few days ago, but that wasn't likely. "We'll go slow and be careful."

We got out, each of us donning our helmets.

Daze didn't complain about his being too big or smelly this time. We quickly made our way out the door and up the stairs without incident. On twelve, I placed my ear to the door and listened. When I was sure it was clear, I eased it open, and we slipped into the hallway.

There were no seekers and no sounds of anyone moving around.

It was eerily quiet.

For the second day in a row, the drizzle had been incredibly light, so even the rain wasn't making its usual racket. Any more days like this, and we'd have to start wearing our air masks. When the rain cleared, on those few sporadic days, the iron dust made it hard to breathe, and no one wanted that crap to settle in their lungs.

"It's all clear. Let's go," I told Daze, who'd stuck behind me, no more than a meter between us.

We made it to the beam. There was leftover damage from the seekers in the form of holes in the walls and more debris than usual kicked around, along with a bit of blood smeared on the walls, but nothing major had been disrupted. Daze grabbed on to the bottom of my vest without being asked, and I stepped out onto the steel girder that would take us to the next building, my hands rising above my head to cling to the rope strung above for this very reason.

Twenty-three steps and we were on the other side.

Before I jumped down, I stopped at the edge, removing my helmet to listen. This was where we'd run into Darby. He'd been in the area, lured here by Tandor's men to work on a cure for Plush. Darby hadn't divulged the exact location of the lab to me, but it was close. I didn't hear any telltale noises. No scuffling and no other movement.

I jumped off the beam, turning to grab Daze's arm to steady him as he followed me down. Then I placed my helmet back on my head and drew out my Gem. Just to be on the safe side, I gestured for Daze to stick behind me. He didn't make a peep.

We passed the room I'd hauled the kid into when I'd heard the noise that turned out to be Darby, and continued to the other end. The stairwell that led to the roof, which, in turn, led to my residence in the canals, was on the right. We continued by without stopping and came to another open window and another beam.

Once again, Daze held on to my waist, no questions asked. This one was longer. I harnessed my Gem, because I would need both hands to grip the line.

Thirty-four steps and we were across.

We traversed one more rafter before we hit the final building. The one that housed six. I hadn't been in this particular area in a while, so I took it slow. Once on the ground, I slid off my helmet, this time setting it on the floor and tucking it under the entrance to the beam. If all went well, I wouldn't need it until we exited, which would take us back this way.

I helped Daze down, and he deposited his helmet next to mine. Reaching into my vest, I took out my chromes. Once I had my Gem positioned in front of us, we crept down the hallway, Daze at my back, my free hand angled behind me, making contact with his shoulder in case I had to grab him and scurry him to safety.

This building was significantly bigger than the last two. It'd been one of the original megascrapers, the second to be built in the city. The base flared wider than subsequent scrapers built in the following years, taking up four city blocks. The floor we were on had held industry and offices. Ten stories above us, around the twenty-second floor, the residences would've begun.

But this building had been sheared off at twenty stories, so all of the residences had been decimated.

It would've been interesting to see what they had looked like in one of the original megascrapers. But, unfortunately, we'd never get that chance.

Six was at the other end, two flights up.

After what seemed like an incredibly long walk—which it was, since the hallway was at least half a block long—we made it to the stairwell. Normally, if Lockland had been monitoring us, there would've been a light telling us if all was clear.

But he was currently indisposed.

I pressed my finger to my lips, indicating to Daze that he should be extra quiet, even though it wasn't needed. The kid had an impressive ability to keep silent. It was a skill set not everyone had.

I knew he was fearful of what was to come. Hell, I was fearful. If Tandor's men had the ability to blow up my residence, there was no reason why they couldn't blow up this building with us standing in it.

Leaning forward, I angled my ear in the direction of the stairwell.

Before I could detect if it was safe or not, the door jerked open. I sprang back, knocking Daze to the ground. My finger almost engaged the trigger of my Gem when I recognized the familiar shape and the grunts that came next. I dropped my arms. "What the fuck, Bender? I almost killed you!"

Chapter 16

I stood, huffing and puffing, my back against the wall, still recovering from almost searing a hole through a family member. Daze stumbled to his feet and came to stand by my side. I ran a shaky hand through my hair. My fingers got irritatingly stuck. I yanked them away, cursing. "Seriously," I cried, "what were you thinking? Why would you just yank open the door like that? Nobody does that."

"I was coming to find you. It was getting late," he answered gruffly. He knew how close he'd just come to getting a laser straight through his abdomen. "Don't worry about it. I'm not dead. I survived. Stop wasting time. Let's go." He braced the door open so we could pass through.

Pushing off the wall shakily, I followed Bender up the two flights that would take us to six, Daze trailing us.

"What's going on?" I asked when I finally found my

composure. "Where did you guys go? I've been worried sick."

"I'll tell you everything once you get inside." Over his shoulder, he grumbled, "We're being hunted."

"I know," I replied. "They came after me, too." Lockland and Bender likely didn't know that one of my residences had literally been blown apart.

Bender held the door open, and Daze and I entered the hallway. Six was down on the right. Bender led the way. We were almost to the door when it sprang open.

It was good I didn't have my Gem drawn this time.

"Darby!" I surprised us both by drawing him into a quick embrace. It took him a second to hug me back, the sensation new for both of us. I wasn't a hugger. Like, really not. But it was so damn good to see him.

After about three seconds, I pushed him out to arm's length. His clothing was slightly askew. "What in the hell happened to you?" I asked. "How did the government get their hands on you? And don't ever open a door like that again! I could've blown your face off."

From behind, Bender growled, "Get inside, and we'll tell you the rest."

I walked into the room, hoping to see Claire, but it was empty. This particular room had no outside windows and was lit by a handful of small lights mounted on the walls. There were four sleeping pallets, a cooling unit, and a few other essentials, including a door that led into a makeshift waste room, which had been a storage closet once upon a time. It was enough to survive, but calling it comfortable was a stretch.

"Where's Lockland?" I asked as Bender shut and secured the door. This was a fairly defensible location, with an escape hatch through the waste room floor, but it wasn't incredibly secure. Staying here for a long period of time wouldn't be advisable. "How come we're here instead of a level-three hold?" Which basically meant underground.

"Most of our locations have been compromised," Bender answered with a growl.

My gaze shot to Darby, who was busy staring at the floor. "I didn't mean to divulge everything, I swear." He shuffled his feet. "The Babble dose they gave me was strong. I had no choice."

I headed over to one of the three chairs and sat. This was going to be a lengthy discussion. Daze followed, opting to make do on the pallet next to me. "I thought the person who received Babble didn't know what they confessed."

Darby looked miserable as he took his own seat. He set his head in his hands. "They recorded it," he groaned. "Then gleefully played it back for me. Partly to terrorize me and partly to get more answers." He lifted his head. "But that was good, I guess. That way I knew exactly what I'd told them and what I didn't. I didn't say anything about this location, because they didn't ask specifically. Anything they asked about, I babbled. That stuff plays for keeps. Listening to myself saying all those things was awful. It was like some other guy posing as me." He shuddered. "I didn't even know they'd been giving it to me. That's the worst part. I'd go to the lab, then go home never knowing anything had happened."

I tensed, expecting the worst. "Did you tell them about my residence in the canals?"

His face brightened. "You hadn't taken me there yet. They knew you had a place there, so they pressed me for details. They even threatened to kill me. I ended up giving them vague directions about the area, swearing I'd never been there, which I hadn't. Then, when they picked me up shortly after we parted ways a few days ago, they'd run out of Babble, so they couldn't inject me." He grinned. "They sent someone out to the general area, and they got caught in one of your traps. They were so pissed. It was perfect."

I'd spied that one of my traps had gone off when I'd gone to my residence with Case to get extra bombs. "I'm relieved they ran out of Babble. That was an incredibly lucky break. It won't be safe to go back home until these guys are completely handled, but it's a huge relief." I scooted forward. "So, how'd you get from Tandor's group into government hands?"

He shrugged, his face back to looking miserable. "I don't know. I think Marta—the fellow scientist I was working with—must have knocked me out with something. She was the only one around once the goons who took me left. When I came to, I was in a small room. It took a day before anyone came to find me. When they did, they had government uniforms on.

They asked me some strange questions about the work I was doing. I made up some stuff, and that's when Claire came in. She pretended to be in charge of my case and broke me out."

"Why isn't she with you now?" I couldn't help but be worried about my friend.

"She had to go back so they wouldn't suspect it was her. She couldn't tell me a lot, but she said really big things were happening on the inside, and there was going to be a shakeup of some kind coming soon. She was anxious to get back so she could be there to aid anyone in need."

"Please tell me she got back safely." I glanced from Darby to Bender. A simple nod from either of them would be fine.

"As far as I know, she did," Darby said. "She's the one who got a hold of Lockland and gave him the coordinates to find me after she broke me out. She and some guy named Mattie took me to this deserted building and dropped me off. It was a government-sanctioned area where they used to do experiments outside the city. It was pretty creepy."

"Is that why you guys left so quickly?" I asked Bender, who stood against the door, his arms crossed. "Claire told you to go pick up Darby?"

He nodded. "She said if we didn't get to him within an hour, his location could be compromised. We wasted no time."

I stood and began to pace in the small enclosure as I told them what had happened to me over the last few hours. "Not all of Tandor's men are gone. In fact, the second in charge, Hutch, is alive and well. There's a distinct chance he purposely stayed out of the fray, knowing Tandor was at a disadvantage." I turned, dropping my hand from where it had crept to my forehead. "They blew up my fucking residence in The North." Darby appeared surprised by the news, but Bender's lips remained pursed in a thin line. "You knew?"

"Heard about it on the way back." Bender inclined his head. His way of giving me sympathy.

"That's not all," I said. "Waiting for Lockland might be advisable, though, since it's serious, and I don't want to have to repeat it." I headed back over to the chair I'd vacated. "By the way, where is he?"

Bender answered, "The assholes had us in their sights once we got back within the city limits. They were waiting for us. Lockland dropped me and Darby off where we'd stashed my craft, and then he led them on a chase. They took the bait. He should be here momentarily."

Darby nodded at Daze. "Nice to see you again, kid. I heard you had a rough ride. But kudos to you for hanging in there." If Darby could've reached him, he would've given Daze a good-natured sock on the arm.

"Thanks," Daze replied, his voice not much more than a whisper. "I couldn't have done it without Holly. She saved my life."

"Yeah, she tends to do that," Darby agreed. "Then we end up owing her big-time. It's a vicious cycle."

I chuckled. "Yeah, right. You'd owe me anyway." Now was as good a time as any to bring out the prize. Waiting for Lockland was getting old. Slowly, I unzipped my vest and reached inside. Darby's eyebrows rose as I slid the pico out, setting it on my lap nonchalantly, like I always carried a superfast computer tucked inside my vest.

Darby sprang out of his seat. "No way!" His gaze shot to mine, his eyes wide. Then he glanced at the pico, then back at me. His hands reached out of their own accord, only to recoil, as if he was unsure that what he was seeing was real. It was an interesting, dramatic response. I hadn't expected any less from Darby. This was a big deal in our world. "The guys that took me kept talking about it," Darby said excitedly. "They needed the quantum drive back bad. They said that without it they wouldn't be able to implement whatever dastardly plan they had cooked up, which they didn't share. But from what I overheard through bits of conversation, it had to do with Plush and infecting innocent people."

I opened up the top and powered it on. The screen jumped to life within seconds. Darby dragged a chair over as I arranged the pico to face him. Daze took his place over my right shoulder. "From what I can surmise," I started, "the documents on here originated from Bliss Corp. I believe it might be the chemical makeup for Plush, as well as a cure—or something like that. Whatever it is, the government was involved." I glanced at Darby, who was completely focused on the screen, barely listening to my awesome explanation. "I couldn't really make sense of it, but I know you can." Carefully, I lifted the pico and set it in his lap. He was momentarily stunned, his jaw going slack, his eyes glazing over. I chuckled. "Darb, I know this is a lot to take in, but it might be a good idea to come back down to Earth." I snapped my fingers in front of his face. "After you look over this, we'll have a lot to discuss. I'm sure you'll keep everything safe while it's in your possession."

He nodded, his eyes refocusing. "I will. I promise." He leaned forward, instantly absorbed by what was in front of him, his fingers busy on the keys.

He'd be lost for a while, and that was fine with me.

I glanced at Bender, who seemed distracted, only mildly interested in the pico and the information we'd uncovered. I stood to walk over, murmuring, "What's the plan if Lockland doesn't return?"

Before Bender could answer, a noise sounded from the hallway. We both backed up, grabbing our weapons. A familiar knock came on the door a minute later.

Bender whipped it open, and Lockland breezed through.

His jacket was torn, and there was blood on his cheek. I harnessed my Gem. "What the hell happened to you?" I asked.

He glanced quickly around the room, taking stock. Once he was satisfied, he turned back to me. "Led those assholes all over the city before I ditched them," he answered, his breathing labored. "They blew up your residence."

"Yeah, I know," I said. "Case and I almost died in the blast. They didn't detonate until we were on our way out. Eventually, we circled back to try and track them down, but the old man who likely exposed our location was dead. He'd been murdered a short time before we arrived." I wasn't going to question how everyone knew it'd been my residence. Gossip traveled fast, and it was obvious the bad guys were proud of their accomplishments. "Even worse news, these guys seem to have taken over Port Station, possibly as long as two months ago. Not sure if all the guards are compromised, but we narrowly escaped with Luce." I began to wander around the tiny room, but I was a pro at navigating without much space. When I was stressed, there was no standing still. "I'm not getting why we didn't know this was going on in our city. It doesn't make any sense. There are clues all over. How did we miss something this big?" Lockland gave Darby a cursory glance as he moved forward, absorbing what was on the techie's lap as he took off his helmet and set it on a pallet.

"We didn't know because the network is closed," Lockland answered as he took a seat, a gloved hand running back and forth over his short hair. "Meaning anyone who's caught talking, or even thinks about talking, dies. They threatened them with Plush, and it's working. I finally got a few people to talk, but only after I promised that what I had in mind would be a lot worse than a dose of Plush." After a moment, he stood and walked over to Darby, positioning himself over his shoulder so he could read what was on the screen.

I continued to move around the room. "They're not only threatening them with it, they're doing it. I ran into two guys in The North, and shortly thereafter, a seeker emerged. The one guy, Dill, was unaffected by her presence. He produced a dart and slammed it into her forehead. He called her Mary. The other guy, Ned, told me that he'd give me some information in exchange for protection. We didn't get a chance to broker a deal, because Dill called him away. I didn't stick around to see what the dart did to Mary, other than knock her out. But that proves that they're using the drug already."

Darby's head came up, his brows furrowed. "I've only perused a few pages so far, but if what's in here is for real, they had the beginnings of a cure for Plush before the meteor hit." He shook his head. "So there's a possibility that all the stuff I was doing in the lab with Marta wasn't a ruse like I thought." He met my gaze. "I think they actually needed my help. It was…real." He stumbled to stand, clutching the pico precariously in his grip.

"Whoa, there," I said, rushing forward, taking the supercomputer out of his hands before he dropped it. Once I had it, I soothed, "It's okay, Darby. You've been through a lot. Sit down." I gently guided him back into his seat by the shoulder. "If the lab was real and the work you were doing was genuine, there's a good chance your work is still there. But if they're smart, they're guarding it, so we have to be careful." When he looked somewhat mollified and refocused, I set the pico back in his lap, keeping my hand on his shoulder. "I need you to stay awake for this, Darb. No passing out. There's a lot of work that needs to be done. Once you get through these documents, we need to make sense of them. You're the only one who can do it."

He looked up at me and nodded. "I will. But I want you to know this is…huge." He glanced back down at the pico and started, like he was surprised to see it sitting there. "From what it says here, the sooner you can get the cure injected, the effects of Plush on the user will vanish to almost nothing." He squinted down at the screen. "It says if it's administered within forty-eight hours, there will be no lasting side effects. For those who have been taking Plush for years, they would need a steady, repetitive dose. It's unclear if they can become completely free of symptoms or not, but that's what I believe Marta was trying to do. She was trying to find the full cure." His voice caught in the back of his throat. "She had…patients. I don't know if she left them there." He tried to stand again, but my hand was still on his shoulder.

Squatting next to him, so we were at eye level, I said, "We can't go check now. Everything you're saying matters. All of us know this is a big deal. But first we have to take care of the threat. If we can't get rid of Hutch and his men, we have no chance of ending this for good. Do you understand what I'm saying?

First, we eliminate the source of the trouble, then we work on a cure for Plush." He nodded, his pupils partially dilated. I leaned forward, our faces close. I could see all the emotion roiling beneath the surface. "Darby, I know you care about this more than anything. You also have a tendency to go nonverbal and get distracted, but I need you to stay in the here and now. You're going to remain here with Daze and work on this research, while Bender, Lockland, and I take care of the threat. Are we clear?"

"Yes."

I patted him on the arm as I stood. "Good. Now we just have to find them."

Chapter 17

We'd been discussing plans for several hours. Blackout was set to begin soon and we were getting ready to move. I was reclined on a pallet, Daze asleep next to me. Darby hadn't stopped his perusal of the pico the entire time, occasionally making nonsensical comments to assure us he was still cognizant of his surroundings.

"Say that again, Darby." I sat up. "What about seventeen?"

He glanced at me, startled that I'd addressed him. "Um, I'm not sure. What was I talking about?"

I scooted to the edge of the makeshift bed, trying not to disrupt Daze. It didn't work. The kid woke, scrambling up quickly. "You mumbled something about The North, then said, 'Stupid seventeen.' You were talking about our safe house, right?" My heart beat quickly as I stood. "What are you reading? It can't say anything about our safe houses in there."

"Oh, it doesn't," he answered nonchalantly. "It's a reflex I've developed from having Babble in my bloodstream. Sometimes I repeat things I said while under the influence of the drug. I don't know why. It must be my brain recalling a memory. I hope it doesn't last long."

I stopped in front of him. "Darby, this is important. I have to know why you were talking about seventeen." I'd told the guys about Cozzi's strange behavior, but we hadn't dwelled on it. "Did you tell Tandor's men about seventeen specifically? I didn't think you'd ever been there." Before all this, Darby had rarely left home.

He nodded. "I went to seventeen once a few years ago. I was picking up a package in The North. I'd bartered some coin for a specialized battery I needed. I got a little scared, and it was getting close to blackout, so I used it." He visibly shuddered. "But I wouldn't do it again. That place is scary. It's so dark and dank."

And currently home to a gentle old man who had a penchant for wearing burial shrouds.

"I have to go," I announced to the group, turning in a semicircle.

Bender was already standing. Lockland got off his chair. They understood my angst without me having to explain it. If Cozzi was in imminent danger, he was the current priority.

"It's time for us all to move," Lockland said. "We're done here. The plan is to gather intel and regroup in three hours. Once we have their known location, we formulate a better, concrete plan. We have enough firepower to take them out—granted, if we can find them. I'm fairly certain I can get the same informants to talk. I'll know more in an hour or two."

I didn't love leaving Darby and Daze alone in six, but it was the only solution. I pulled my taser off my waist and walked over to Daze. "Here you go, kid." I set it in his outstretched hand. It was so big that his fingers didn't reach all the way around the handle as he grasped it. "It's set to full tase. Your job is to stay here and protect Darby and the pico at all costs. I showed you the way out through the floor in the waste room already." I'd also explained how to get to my residence in the canals from here and how to maneuver through my traps. Darby hadn't been listening, but the kid had been all ears. "If you have to evacuate, get to my residence. Do you remember everything I told you?" The kid nodded, his face serious, even though it was still creased with sleep.

"I can do it." He stuck the taser in his waistband. It looked ridiculously large next to his bony body.

"I know you can," I said. "That's why I'm putting you in charge."

"When we leave here, flip this," Bender said, pointing to a switch on the wall. "It actives the lasers outside the door. Anybody coming through this way gets sliced."

Lockland moved forward. "But that doesn't mean you stay if there's trouble. Get out as soon as possible. Follow Holly's directions and use the tech phone she gave you. Try all four channels. Someone will be there." My heart gave a squeeze to hear my crew giving Daze directions that would save his scrawny hide. They cared what happened to him. That spoke volumes, and I knew Daze was listening.

Bender opened the door, and he and Lockland went through. I followed, glancing back. "Darby, make sure you and the kid stay alive. If Tandor's men have infected even half as many people as I think they have, we're going to need that cure."

"Will do," he answered. "I'm pretty sure Marta had access to most of the compounds listed here. I just have to get over to the lab to see." His eyes shone with excitement.

"We'll head over first thing when I get back, but not a moment before. Do you hear me?" I had to clear my throat to get his attention, which he had refocused on the pico. "Darby, do you understand? We don't go to the lab until I get back. It's too dangerous for you and Daze to go alone. I don't care how close it is."

"Yes, yes, I understand."

That was all I was getting. I nodded to Daze. "Stay safe. Use the phone if you need to."

"I will," he said. "Holly?" I gave him my attention. "Stay safe." The kid was putting on a brave face, and I appreciated that.

"That's the plan," I said, giving him a smile and a three-finger salute as I slipped out the door, shutting it firmly behind me. Bender was already in the stairwell, Lockland waiting in the hallway.

We made excellent time, arriving where I'd left

Luce in less than twenty minutes, which was a record for me.

"Where's your craft?" I asked Bender as we entered the secured room.

He jammed his thumb behind him. "Next building, old parking ramp."

I popped Luce's door. "You want a lift?" Lockland walked around to Luce's passenger side and got in.

Bender snorted. "Like the three of us would fit in there. After you leave, I'll lock up. See you in three." He held up the last three fingers of his right hand. "We regroup then."

I chuckled as I got in. "Are you saying my craft is small?" I flipped my visor up since the lights were on.

"A1's are puny."

"Hey, careful now." I started her up. The plan was for Lockland and me to travel to The North together. Once we arrived, we were each going our separate ways to try to find as much information as we could on Hutch, Cozzi being my first stop, tracking down Ned my second. Bender was heading to The Middle to start actively shaking down his contacts. It was pretty incredible that Bender hadn't heard any trickle-down about Tandor's men either. And to say he wasn't happy about it was a gross understatement.

I'd pity his neighbors, but I didn't have any to spare.

"Expect a fight," Bender said. "You're heading right into the heart of trouble. Watch your back."

Bender had tried to talk me out of going to see

about the old man, but I had demurred. Once I made sure Cozzi was all right, I could focus, but not until then. Lockland had offered his assistance, but traveling as one was far more discreet than traveling as two. I needed to be stealthy if I was going to intercept Ned without the Dillweed catching on.

We'd all agreed to keep in contact via the tech phone twice an hour. "I'm not planning on dying anytime soon," I told him. "Cozzi's going to talk whether he wants to or not, and so will Ned. Once I have that information, I'll make contact."

"If you find yourself in a bind and we can't get there, give Militia a call," Bender said, backing up as I reached up to grab Luce's door.

"Are you giving me permission to let Case in on our plans?" I asked, giving him a pissy look. I'd shared everything that happened with them, including Case's backstory. I turned to Lockland. "Are you in agreement with him? We're choosing to trust Case now? Because if we are, I might have an issue with that. The guy told me some stuff, but he hasn't proven anything to us yet. The entire story could be bullshit."

"What Bender is saying is the guy could be an asset in a fight. If you're in trouble, call those who offer help. For now, that's us and Militia." He grinned, showing straight, white teeth. He was a lucky man. "I've heard stories about the mysterious Dixon. I don't think Case was lying. Dixon's got quite a rep and is well known in certain circles. Though I'd thought he died a while ago, but apparently not." Lockland sounded impressed, which surprised me even more than the guys telling me to call Case if I needed assistance.

"We'll see," I grumbled as I closed the door. I wasn't letting either of them know Case had no access to a phone, so it was a moot point. Bender saluted as I hit the button to open the wall. The graphene in front of us began to part immediately. Once outside, we would fly parallel to the city and then enter just before The North began. Knowing Hutch and his men were on the lookout, it was too risky to take the streets. "You know, suddenly deciding to trust this guy after a fifteen-minute discussion about where he came from seems a little premature to me." I lofted Luce into the air, letting Bender shut things up from the inside.

"It's not just the story," Lockland said. "Although it helped. This guy has aided us a few times. Only takes one more, and he's in."

I balked, gliding Luce low along the tree line to keep her out of sight. "How can you say that?" I turned to make sure Lockland could see my bewildered expression. "I'm positive the guy's been holding back the entire time. He knows more than he's ever let on. That sob story he fed me easily could've been a lie. There's no way to know for certain, and now he gets the third-time's-the-charm rule? I don't think so." Case hadn't earned our collective trust yet. Far from it.

"I agree. He could still be playing both sides, but if he is, he's doing it for a reason. If he ends up double-crossing us, I'd be surprised. If he was Dixon's man, he's the focused type who would continue seeking justice for his nephew. That means taking Tandor's entire crew out. That's the way it goes. And you know as well as I do that if someone saves one of our lives more than twice, they're in."

This discussion was pissing me off. There was something about Case that didn't ring true. Playing both sides didn't surprise me, but there was more. The man knew too much. He'd tracked me too easily in The North. He managed to get me to bring him back to my place. The residence I no longer had.

We'd find out soon enough, because when shit got real with Hutch and his men, everything would shake out.

"Are you sure you don't want me to take you to your ride?" I asked. Lockland had abandoned his craft after the chase and come to the canals on foot.

"Nope. They had to have found her by now. I rigged her with traps. If they try anything, they're going to pay for it. We should enter The North on foot. Once we separate, I won't be that far away. If you need me, just reach out."

"I will. I'm not expecting to get caught, but if I do, I'll ring the alarm."

"This guy Hutch has to be smarter than Tandor, which makes sense since he's still alive. Like Bender said, watch your back. Expect them to be sneaky."

"Sneaky and sloppy." I chuckled. "So far, we've managed to evade everything they've thrown at us. We killed Tandor and took out at least half their crew. As far as I'm concerned, we're going to come out on top because we don't make mistakes like they do. If we're trying to blow someone up, we get the job done."

"That's true," Lockland said as I pushed Luce faster. We'd arrive at our destination very soon. I planned to enter the city at a location I wasn't familiar with, but Lockland was. "But we can't forget that they managed to do something nobody's ever done before—they kept themselves cloaked in *our* city." His words came out in a snarl. "They orchestrated how and when we found out about them and played the advantage as long as they could. It would've worked, too, if the kid hadn't stolen the quantum drive and forced their hand. He deserves a reward."

I hadn't thought about it before, but Lockland was right. What Daze had done had made Tandor stumble out into the open. Whether the kid had planned it or not, it'd been a brilliant move. I'd have to find a suitable reward once this was all over.

Something shiny and weapony.

Lockland shook his head as he continued, "We can't afford to make this kind of a mistake again. I'm going to have to find more contacts and enhance our security measures. Get ready to do some serious salvaging. I'm going to have a long list of supplies we're going to need."

"Tell me about it," I said. "With one of my residences gone, I'm depleted more than what's comfortable. It's a huge relief that Darby didn't blab about my place in the canals. If he had, I'd be wiped out." It was still hard to think about the loss of my home. "Now that I have a kid hanging around, needing stuff like food and a roof over his head, it makes it a little more intense. I can't afford to be without resources."

"Three buildings down, go up and over the wall," Lockland directed. "Nobody monitors here, but as soon as you're over, drop down immediately and take a right. They won't be expecting us to resurface before morning." He grinned, his teeth gleaming in the low light. "But that doesn't mean they don't have people on watch."

I did as Lockland asked, going up over the wall that had been built around the city following the dark days. It'd been for both stabilization and protection, but it was hardly monitored anymore. The government had more important things to do, like arrest and interrogate innocent people. Though, they did enjoy sending out their UACs to try to keep people in line.

I hadn't seen a government drone in weeks, which was strange.

Once we were in, even though I was flying without headlights, I could tell where we were. It was a fairly desolate area, most of the buildings crumbling beyond repair. No one lived here. It was outside of any protected area and, for the most part, unsafe and uninhabitable. There were a lot of pockets like this in the city. These were the down places that separated the neighborhoods.

I wanted to set Luce down as soon as possible, because props were loud and attracted attention.

"That building up on the left, the one that's sheared off at four stories?" Lockland said, gesturing out the windshield. "I've used it before. There's a hollowed-out place on the first floor. The opening's small, but you shouldn't have an issue getting to it. The entrance is up and over some tall rubble, so it will keep the craft cloaked."

"Got it," I said. "I've used a building up on the right, but I usually park on the roof. I'm thinking lower is better, because we might need to make a quick exit."

He nodded. "First-floor access would be a plus."

I glided into the space Lockland had indicated. The opening wasn't much bigger than craft size, but doable. I set her down immediately. Turning her off, I glanced around with my visor down, searching for any heat signatures that shouldn't be here. "Seems pretty secure. I'll have to remember this for next time." If there was a next time. Honestly, once this was over, I'd happily take a hiatus from The North for a good long time.

We both got out, crunching over rock and debris toward the opening, which was up a slight hill made of crumbled concrete. Lockland gestured as he made his way toward the right. "There's a short trail. A long time ago, I tried to make it into some stairs, but it didn't work. The debris is too loose."

We hurried, slipping and sliding, but finally managing to conquer the mound. At the top, we both stilled, listening for any strange noises. "Sounds clear to me," I whispered. "Do you have a preferable way to enter from here?"

"Two blocks straight ahead, there's a building that's habitable, but only above the fifth story. It should be quiet about now, and it has a pass-through."

I nodded. "Sounds good to me." I kept my voice low as we moved down the rubble from the other side, which went quicker than climbing up, and entered the street. "I always use the entrance a kilometer east of here. It's the closest point of entry to my now-defunct residence." I made a grumbling noise that ended up coming out like a strangled cough. "No one monitors it. It's the one with the big painted sign."

Lockland drew his weapon of choice. "I know that entrance. I've used it once or twice." His gun was a Blaster, a wicked-looking thing a little bigger than his fist and heavy as hell. It shot large explosive cartridges full of scrap tungsten. Meaning it exploded sharp, nasty, jagged chunks of metal into your body, essentially ripping it to shreds. There was no surviving a blast, which was why it was sometimes referred to as a Death Blaster. I drew out my Gem. She was equally as wicked, but I liked to think it was in a different, more eloquent and searing kind of way. I tried carrying a Blaster for a while, but the thing was so big it hurt my wrist to keep it upright.

"Here we go." Lockland slid his back along a building, his head methodically moving as he scanned the area.

I followed him closely. "Let's hope this ends tonight."

"There's a good chance things will come to completion sooner than later," he agreed.

"Just the way I like it."

Chapter 18

Lockland was right, the building had a pass-through, and it was empty—though we had to break a pretty hefty lock to gain access. I was a competent lock picker, but having tech aids at my disposal made it easier. A concentrated laser slice, and it'd popped right open.

Once on the other side, we parted ways.

We could do more damage and gather more intel—not to mention be less conspicuous—if we were apart. It was risky, but it was the right thing to do.

From this location, I was a kilometer and a half away from seventeen and Cozzi.

As I jogged, sticking to the side routes I knew were uninhabited, I prayed the old man was still alive. If he wasn't, I was directly responsible for his death. I'd pretty much manhandled him down there in his shroud, dragging his possessions along with us.

It didn't take me long to traverse the distance.

I'd seen a few people, but I'd stuck to the shadows. I was lucky no one had noticed me. Ten meters before the opening of the building where Cozzi was, I heard voices.

"Damn," I swore under my breath. The talking was coming from the interior. I slipped closer, moving like a ghost. They didn't have anyone guarding the outside. Another mistake.

I listened at the edge of the entrance.

One of the voices sounded familiar.

It was Dill, and he was issuing orders. "I don't give a fuck how long it takes," he shouted, his voice agitated. "She'll come back here to get that old man. It might be a day or might be three. You will intercept her when she does. Take her alive. Hutch needs that quantum drive back, or we can't go along as planned. So, you stay here, don't complain, and you get your fucking job done. If I have to come back, I'll kill you both and replace you. Or better yet, you can just become my Plushies." Footsteps headed out. They were moving quickly. I ducked around the corner just in time, praying the asshole would turn my way. I was itching to make him hurt. The fact he hadn't recognized me on the street when we'd met earlier should've been enough to get him killed—or at least kicked out of the dictatorship. Maybe Ned hadn't told him who I was.

Instead of heading toward me, however, the footsteps faded in the opposite direction. Well, there would certainly be a next time.

Cozzi was my first priority. My fear for the old man's well-being thumped in my chest.

I crept back to my former spot outside the building. Dill was nowhere in sight. I angled my head, my ear positioned to better hear what the guards were saying. There were two voices.

"Hutch has a new nickname for him," one guy cracked.

"Yeah, what's that?" the other said.

"Dillweed," he snickered.

"I don't get it."

I rolled my eyes.

"I didn't at first either, but he said it was some kind of plant." He snickered again. "A lowly plant that died off a long time ago."

"That's not funny."

It was totally funny.

These guys were definitely not too bright. I had no idea how much firepower they had or if they were wearing armor. My Gem could penetrate most things, but if they wore something highly reflective, there could be some refraction, which could prove deadly if the surface was shiny enough.

Either way, I didn't have a choice.

I drew my Gem and my HydroSol, which shot hydrogen-air bullets. If they connected with the bloodstream, they were fatal, but the gun was loud and would alert anyone in the area that I was here. I thought better of it and put the air gun back and drew out one of my knives.

Once the two of them were distracted by trying to interpret some of the markings on the wall, I stepped inside, dodging debris to keep quiet. One was quite a bit larger than the other. I needed him down first. If I could get the other guy to talk, that would be the best scenario.

Creeping up behind them, I casually murmured, "Hey."

They both spun around at the same time, fumbling for their weapons.

I was quicker.

My Gem blasted a hole through the big guy's upper arm, and my knife landed in the other one's thigh. They both went down. I moved quickly, knocking the big guy unconscious with the butt of my weapon. Then I straddled the other guy, ripping the knife out of his thigh and placing it at his neck. "I need you to stop making noise now," I growled. He complied as best he could, a whimper or two still wheezing through. "Consider yourself lucky to be alive. Tell me what's going on, and you'll continue breathing." After a few more mewls, I pressed the tip of the knife in, drawing blood. "Why are you here?"

"Because…because," he sputtered, "you're coming for the old man, right? That's why you came, didn't you?" He grimaced in pain as he inadvertently moved, causing my blade to dip farther in. My knife was serrated, so it wouldn't be a clean cut. "I'm not with them, I swear." He began babbling, "They made me do it. They didn't have enough men, so they went into the skells. They threatened us with Plush. Me and my boyo over there, we don't know these guys. We don't owe them any allegiance. They said they'd infect us!"

My knife remained in his neck. "Why comply? Why not just leave?"

He looked confused, his eyebrows furrowing. "And go where? There ain't anyplace else to go. And these guys said that they would find us. Said they were going to be the new government, and if we didn't follow their orders, we would be their slaves. And they have slaves, too. I seen them! They're like seekers, but different. They can control them. It's creepy as shit. But we know you. And your crew. I'll do anything you want. Please don't kill me." His hands began to slide up in a surrender pose.

"Don't do that." My voice was hard. He stopped instantly. I had to decide if he was telling the truth or not, which was always tricky. "What's your name?"

"Willy," he answered quickly. "I was born above Rothman skell. Have you heard of it? My mama and daddy lived there. I never left. Got nowhere to go." He was basically right about that. Northerners were born and raised here and rarely left.

"Do you know a guy who goes by the name of Ned?"

He nodded. "Ned works for Dill now. I wouldn't take that job for anything. Dill's a mean son of a bitch."

"Willy, there's no way for me to know if you're telling me the truth or not—"

"I am, I swear!" he insisted.

I shook my head. "Saying it doesn't make it true. I hear what you're telling me, and it makes sense. I don't want to kill you if I don't have to. So I'm going to give you a test. Okay?"

He appeared uncertain. His face was round and full. He couldn't be more than early twenties. "I think so."

"Good, that was exact answer I wanted to hear. Here's what I'm going to do. I'm going to knock you out, and once you come to, I want you to find Ned and give him this message. Are you ready?" Willy began to protest. I cut him off. "We're not making a deal, Willy. This isn't a negotiation. Do what I say, and if you don't, I'll hunt you down, and you won't like what comes next, because it's bound to be really bloody. Are you ready?"

"Yes."

"I want you to tell Ned to meet me in an hour at the same place he first saw me. Do you understand the message? It's extremely simple."

"Yes, but before you knock me out, do you have a numbing agent? My leg hurts real bad."

"No." I struck the side of his skull with my Gem. He went out instantly. I didn't have time to waste. I had to be out by the time he and his friend came to. I hurried down the stairs toward seventeen. As I ran, I could see our traps had been blown left and right. I had to step over a body. This didn't bode well for Cozzi. I kept trying to think of reasons why they would keep him alive, but I couldn't come up with any. He was a defenseless old man, but they would assume I'd told him things, that we were colluding.

I arrived at the end of the hallway.

The door was ajar.

"*No, no, no,*" I whispered as I shouldered it open. Cozzi lay half on the pallet, half off. His face was covered in blood, so much so that I couldn't tell if it was actually him or not. The only thing making me certain was the burial cloth. I rushed to his side, kneeling. "Cozzi, I'm so sorry." I set a hand on an arm that was exposed. "This is not what I intended for you."

I didn't expect him to answer, so I was surprised as hell when he did.

It was a rattling cough at first, followed by a small gasp of air. "It's not your fault," he managed, his voice raspy and ragged. "It's my own damn fault." A few more racking coughs.

I glanced around frantically, searching for something to use to wipe the blood away from his face. The only thing available was the burial shroud he was still wrapped in. I found an edge of the fabric and dabbed the unforgiving material against his face. He cringed, but let me do it. "What happened?" I asked. "Why did they do this to you?"

"They hit me a number of times when I didn't answer the questions the way they liked."

Very gently, I rolled him toward me, transferring his head to my lap. He groaned. I had a feeling the injuries were worse than he was letting on. "What did they want to know?"

"The usual things," he answered. "How I knew you,

where you were"—he coughed—"how come I held out on them."

"They were the reason I found you outside with all your belongings?" I asked. But I already knew the answer. They'd tried to get Cozzi to bend like the guard I'd just interrogated upstairs, but he'd resisted. He was old, so they'd overlooked him the first time and let him go, but not before throwing him out on the street like a pile of garbage. The second time they weren't going to spare him.

"Don't be too mad at me. I'm just a silly old man," he said, his voice wheezy. "If I'd told you about them, you would've gone after them, and you would've endangered yourself. Gone in with guns blazing, I imagine. There are too many. They have means, and they're making seekers. If you got injected with that stuff, there would be nothing you could do. You'd be in a sorry state." He began to cough and couldn't stop, blood slowly leaked out of the corner of his mouth in a thin line, trailing all the way down his chin.

I peeled back the burial shroud. It didn't take long to reveal his ravaged chest. "Oh, Cozzi." I blinked back tears as I lifted my head toward the ceiling, trying to pull myself together. Then I raged, "Those bastards are going to pay for what they did to you. You have my word. They won't get out of this city alive."

He gave me a weak smile. "Promise me one thing, girl. You come back here when you're all done giving them hell and get old Cozzi. I want to be buried at sea, like they did in the ancient times. You take this cloth, wrap me up real tight, and put me on something that floats. I've always dreamt of the sea. I'll make it out to the Flotilla yet." He tried to chuckle, but it set off another series of hacking coughs and wheezes. The trickle of blood increased to a flow, coating his chin.

Irrational ideas popped into my head about trying to get him out of here and to the Medi Center. But I knew he would die. There was nothing I could do about it, nor could anyone. The wound to his chest was fatal. It was a miracle he'd lasted this long.

He was a tough old fart.

I covered him back up, tucking the cloth around his shoulders. He trembled in my arms. "Remember the first time I met you?" I said. "My mother had just died, and I was on the streets for the very first time. Our paths crossed, and you were the oldest person I'd ever seen in my life."

His mouth turned up in a curve, his eyes quieting, his expression slacking. "I remember it clear as day," he uttered on a weak breath. "You waltzed up to me, hands on your hips, and demanded shelter. I thought to myself, 'Whoever messes with this girl will rue the day,' so I let you in. Never felt I had a choice in the matter, really."

I chuckled, remembering it like a hologram replaying in front of my eyes. "I chose you for a reason. And it wasn't because you were the oldest person I'd ever seen." I smiled down on him, a few tears spilling over. "I chose you because of your eyes." The Cozzi of eighteen years ago wasn't that far off from the Cozzi today. He still had the same eyes. They were kind. They were docile. They said specifically, *I won't harm you.*

"My eyes?" he said on the barest of breaths, his eyes fluttering shut.

"They're kind. Just like you."

He tried to give me a smile, his eyelids blinking rapidly as what was left of his chest heaved. There was no air left in his lungs for a cough. Only a bit left to say, "They must look just like yours."

He went still.

I held him tight, my head bowed.

A scream welled in my throat. I felt like ripping this place apart, like finding Hutch, and Dill, and Slim, and everyone else, and obliterating them. The rage washed over me like a thick blanket of hate. Maddening thoughts about every single unfair thing that'd ever happened to me in this godforsaken city raced through my mind.

Instead of throwing a tantrum, I held the man who'd given me shelter, who'd given me a chance at life on more than one occasion, and cried.

The grief was overwhelming.

I had to hold it close. If I let it loose, it would kill me. If I let it rule my actions, I would make mistakes. And if I died, I wouldn't be able to avenge Cozzi and give him the burial he deserved.

I gave myself thirty seconds.

When the moment had passed, I lifted his almost weightless body in my arms and transferred it to the pallet, rearranging what was left of the burial shroud—something he'd known he'd need sooner rather than later—to cover his face. "Rest well, my friend. I hope the other side is filled with sun and sea."

Chapter 19

Rain poured down a little harder than it had this morning. I was positioned on the fourth floor of a building across the street and down a block from the place I'd first run into Dill and Ned. After I'd left Cozzi, the guards were just beginning to regain consciousness, groaning but alive.

They had rung the alarm a short time later, like I'd known they would.

Now I was waiting—not so patiently—for Willy to do what I'd asked him to do. The chances he would follow through with the plan were less than half— okay, more like less than a third. But I had a feeling he would do it. He'd had something in common with Ned, apparent on both of their faces.

Pure desperation.

Life under Hutch, Slim, and Dill would likely be worse than the shitty life they already had to deal with each and every day.

I was their way out.

There had been a flurry of activity after Willy and his boyo had alerted everyone that I was in the neighborhood. The place where I'd seen Dill for the first time wasn't their headquarters, so currently I didn't have a view of any of the action.

A craft buzzed around the corner at a quick clip, moving expertly between the buildings.

I ducked behind a large piece of metal to mask my body temp from infrared. Damn. Getting out of this area without being seen was going to be tricky. I'd give Ned ten more minutes to show, then I was going to have to find a way to disappear and glean information another way.

Trying to keep from being antsy, I crouched down and thought about avenging Cozzi. I didn't do loss well. Everyone knew that. In order to rectify his death, I needed to make sure his sacrifice mattered. That would happen at a bare minimum. The old man had lived a long life in this town—a city that took and rarely gave anything back in return. He'd been a child when the meteor struck, on his own, much like I'd been.

I spotted movement on the street below. Ned was edging toward the meet a block away. Then I detected another body as it ducked behind a pile of debris. Then another. "Oh, Willy. You had to go and make this difficult, didn't you?" There was no doubt that Willy had told whoever was in charge that I'd requested a meeting with Ned, instead of finding and telling only Ned. If Ned could have, he would've met me secretly.

This meeting was compromised.

I slid back into the shadows, deciding on a plan. Did they honestly think I was just going to waltz out there and start up a conversation?

Given how Dill had treated me, they didn't think women were too smart. But still. I'd have to have half a brain to show up. It was insulting.

Once they realized I was a no-show, Ned would have to figure out what to do. If he still wanted protection in exchange for information, he'd have to make a few key decisions. If he had working brain cells, he'd head somewhere without an audience, somewhere that was familiar to us both. "That is, if you have enough of those cells. We shall see."

I cautiously picked my way to the first floor. This building was unstable and uninhabited. There were several ways out. It'd been retail space of some sort, almost all glass. I chose the exit opposite of where Ned and the sneaky goons were gathering. This building was far enough away from the current meeting place, but close enough it should warrant some investigation eventually.

Easing my head out, I did a cursory check.

It was clear.

According to Willy, Hutch had been forced to recruit Northerners because his men had been depleted. Right now, it showed. This place should be crawling with bodies scouring for me, but there was nobody in sight. I headed out on the street, my shoulder so close to the building it brushed against it as I ran.

Four blocks over, even farther away from our meet, I ducked into another storefront. My former blown-out residence was right around the corner.

If Ned wanted to find me, he would head this way. He had to know it was my residence that they'd demolished. It was the only thing that linked us.

I wasn't going to wait for very long, but this space would give me ample cover. Inside, remnants of old merchandise were strewn around, mixed with bits of collapsed shelving and common household supplies, most of them battered and crushed beyond recognition. I stepped over a dozen mangled lighting units and was just about to maneuver over another pile when I noticed the corner of an unfamiliar package peeking out, almost completely covered by heavy debris.

Squatting, I grasped the edge of the packaging and pulled.

It wouldn't budge.

Shifting some of the stuff out of the way, trying not to make any noise, I was finally able to slide it out less than half a meter. It was a hologram camera, still in its original wrapper. The box was barely there, but it was a box nonetheless. It was a sweet find.

After all these years, rarely, if ever, did one find something still in its original packaging. Odds were that it would work with some fine-tuning.

It was too cumbersome to take now. I glanced around, trying to find a better place to store it. Daze would get a kick out of this if we could get it to work. Back before the dark days, everyone used holograms. From what I'd heard, the video quality had been amazing. Some forms of entertainment could even be performed in the middle of your living room.

Finding nowhere better, I tucked it back under where I'd found it, covering it up with more trash. I'd have to take a chance it was still here when I came back.

After I was done, I clapped the grime off my hands and made my way to the side of the building that Ned would likely pass by first, if he took a direct route from where he'd been standing waiting for me on the street.

Picking the most concealed location, I placed my back up against the wall, bending my knees to squat behind a partition that was half standing. From this vantage point, I could see out onto the street at the correct angle, but I was far enough inside to be protected from view. Once I ID'd him, I would have to make it to the other side of the building to intercept him. It was too risky to talk to him here.

Reaching into a pocket, I withdrew a tech phone. "It's Ella," I said, the button depressed, my voice lowered. "Waiting on a friend."

Static, and then, "Copy that. It's Jerry. I'm making the rounds. Likely location is south."

South?

Lockland was telling me that Hutch's headquarters

were in the canals, not in The North. That didn't make any sense. The North was crawling with his guys. Why would he have a pretense of being in The North when he was actually in the canals?

I was just about to ask that very thing, in code, when the static ended and Bender's voice boomed over the line. "It's Johnny." I had to push the phone down into my vest to muffle the sound. "South is correct. Heading there momentarily."

"Got it," I answered. "I'll join you in a few."

I didn't like that Hutch was in the canals. We'd left Darby and Daze there without any backup. If Lockland had gotten information on Hutch's headquarters that quickly, it was likely people in The North were beginning to talk. Tensions must be rising, as this thing—whatever it was—came to a head. There would be factions for and against. If Willy's information meant anything—that those two had been forced to work with Hutch and his crew or else get a dose of Plush—there would be quite a few against.

Impatient didn't come close to how I felt. If Ned didn't surface in three minutes, I was going to scrap the meeting and head south.

Less than a minute later, footsteps sounded, moving toward me at a quick pace. It could be a random person from the neighborhood, maybe one of Hutch's guys investigating the area, or it could be Ned.

I needed a visual as they approached.

Ned's stringy brown hair was a dead giveaway.

He was sans helmet, his hands stuffed in his pockets, head down. He passed my location without glancing in. I waited a few seconds to see if there were any people following him.

If this operation was smart, his tail would be close, but they wouldn't want to spook me. I was going to use that to my advantage and make this meet quick.

I jogged through the building, avoiding the trash as I went, choosing a place that would be in front of Ned as he turned the corner.

If he didn't come this way, it would be a miss, and I'd take that as a warning.

Luckily, I didn't have to wait long before his footsteps echoed toward me again. Right as he arrived at my location, I drew out my Gem, staying immobile in the shadows of the overhang.

I uttered three words as he passed: "Get in here." He started, shocked to see I was actually there. But he masked it quickly. I gestured impatiently. "At least try to make it look like you were heading in here on purpose."

Before he had a chance to respond, I heard noises. More footsteps, like a dozen, and they were running.

Damn it.

Ned shook his head, his eyes downcast. "I'm sorry. I wish it could've been different. This wasn't my intent. When Dill figured out who you were the other morning, he went ballistic. He threatened to make me a slave and to kill anyone who was close to me. I couldn't risk it."

I was already racing the other way. I couldn't overly fault Ned. Had I known what was at stake in the first place, I would've taken him with me the first time we'd met. But hindsight was always crystal clear. That was why it was called hindsight.

Foresight was what I should've had at this very moment.

Fucking foresight.

Running through the building, I had to decide which direction to go once I arrived on the street. It was going to be a chase game no matter what. I was almost there when a voice called out of the shadows, ironically not even a meter from where I'd just stood waiting for Ned.

Dill sauntered into view in front of me, carrying a nasty-looking magnetic pulse gun pointed directly at my chest. It was identical to the one Case had used in Port Station. "Stop right there," he drawled, "or I liquefy your insides and watch them pour out all the holes." Dill had such an eloquent way with words.

I slowed, veering to the right, deciding whether to take my chances. Pulse guns weren't always accurate. Whatever was inside the bullets made them miss a majority of the time. I had a solid chance to outrun him.

"I know what you're thinking," he said, "and that's just stupid. I don't miss." Before I could actually make a decision either way, more footfalls moved toward us, coming from both directions. Shit. Dill grinned, showing a mouthful of yellow teeth. "Now it's time for you to raise those pretty little hands and get to surrendering. And while you're at it, I'll take that vest from you." At least fifteen men filled in around us, most of them with weapons drawn. Ned was one. "Go on, take it off now, before I get pissy," Dill said. "That was mine the moment I saw it."

Very slowly, I lifted my hands. "You take my vest, you die."

He waltzed over slowly, clearly enjoying the show, acting like he already owned the city and everyone in it. He licked his lips in a very deliberate way. Any other scenario, and I would've smashed that grin off his face. "Honey, the only person who's dying around here is *you*." Once he was close enough, he ripped off my helmet, tossing it down with a clatter. Then he stuck the barrel of his gun against the center of my forehead, leaning in so close his tepid breath wafted across my cheeks. "That is, *after* you hand over the goods, like that vest and the drive."

I was unmoved.

Honestly, it was hard to be cowed by a guy like Dill. Because I felt like it, I jammed my forehead against the barrel, causing the asshole to shift backward a step. Why? Because I was stronger. "What?" It came out in a low growl. "You think I just carry the goods on me like some kind of fucking amateur?"

Surprise hit him a second before anger.

He snarled, making an angry jab forward, trying to force my head to comply. He had to use both hands.

I almost snickered as I tilted my neck back to accommodate.

We were engaged in a battle of wits, both of us seeking power and dominance. But Dill had no clue. None whatsoever. Which was why I was going to win.

"You've got a lot of pockets in that pretty thing of yours. I'm thinking someone like you keeps all her goods close to the *vest*."

I gave him a smirk. "How about we find out?"

He flashed his surprise that he was able to get me to acquiesce so easily, his eyes darting around the assembled crowd to see what everyone else thought. Because Dill, the Dillweed, had no cognitive skills.

The group was unhelpful, until one guy called out, "Make her show you!"

Dill's eyes narrowed as he took a step back, his gun still aimed at my head. Damn, a shot to the head would hurt. Not to mention all that liquefying of my insides. "Take that vest off and show me what you got."

"No problem. It's all yours." I tilted my head as I began to unzip the front, making sure I took the zipper down excruciatingly slowly. My eyes swept around the circle, my eyelids fluttering, my smile showing increasingly more teeth as I went. "You boys excited to see what I have in here?"

Once my attention was off Dill, he acted predictably. He reached for the vest, trying to grab hold of it to force me to go faster. I slapped his hand away.

But before he could react, I replied coldly, "Are you trying to kill everyone here, Dill? Because I'm sure the boys would like to live to see another day. And if you don't think I have bombs in here, then you're crazier than I thought. You mishandle this piece of clothing, and we're all going to blow."

Dill huffed, but backed off, his weapon still up. "You will hand us the bombs, real careful. Do anything strange, and you're a dead girl."

I eased the vest over my shoulders, one at a time, my eyes still raking the group. Once it was off, and as slowly as I'd lowered the zipper, I reached into the first pocket, drawing out my tube keys. I held them up, jingling them. "Who wants these?" They all looked confused. When no one stepped forward, I turned to Dill. "Where would you like me to deposit them?"

It was clear Dill hadn't carried out many—if any—interrogations. But that didn't stop him from acting like he had. He jutted his chin to the right. "Set them there on that broken fan." I did as I was told. I pulled out a few more mundane objects—a laser key, a small knife, a super-bright light the size of my thumb tip. I set them all in the designated spot. "Where are the bombs?" he whined. "Why are you taking so long?"

My features crumpled in concentration as I bent my head, becoming increasingly interested in the rest of the pockets, my hands darting in and out of each one. I finally pulled out my tech phone, which Dill promptly swiped out of my hand. "I'll take that. These beauties are hard to come by. Now the bombs."

I turned the vest around, giving it a confused look, then I held it up like a prize. My eyebrows quirked, expressing my confusion. "I must've forgotten to put them in this morning—"

Dill snatched the garment, his face clouding. "You think you can deceive me like that?" *Well, yes, Dill, I do.* "I'll take this and everything else that's in it."

I crossed my arms. "The quantum drive is not in there, asshole. And neither are any bombs. I doubt it'll fit you. You're bigger than I am. That thing was custom-made to my exact body size and shape."

Dill gestured at a guy standing to my right. "Keep your weapon on her." Then he holstered his own and shrugged on the vest, sucking in his stomach as he forced the zipper up. Once it was on, albeit fairly snuggly, he slapped his chest with both hands, making a loud clapping noise. "Looks like you're wrong, little honey. Fits just fine. I guess it was custom-made for *me.*"

"Looks like it."

Pissed that his actions didn't get more of a reaction out of me, he ripped his gun back out of its holster, waving it at me. "You're going to turn around and walk onto the street real slow. There's a craft waiting outside. We're going to bind you up nice and tight, then deliver you like a present to Hutch and Slim. Then we can finally get this show on the road." He let out a large whoop, like he alone was in charge of the party.

I turned and followed the men out.

A grin on my face.

Chapter 20

True to Dill's word, they bound me up without a centimeter to spare. Steel grips encircled my wrists, which were secured in front of my body. They even added a nice, smelly face mask to make the prisoner ensemble complete. It was someone's old shirt, and it reeked. I couldn't fault Daze any longer for thinking my crap smelled. I'd be lucky if I could keep the scant contents in my stomach down.

The stench was unreal.

They'd stuffed me into the passenger seat, Dill at my back, the butt of his gun shoved uncomfortably into my shoulder. I had no idea who was piloting. He or she hadn't said a word since we'd gotten in.

"Where are we going?" I asked, not caring if I got a response, just needing to do something.

"To the Emporium," Dill answered proudly, like it was world-renowned and I should know what the hell he was talking about.

There were several Pleasure Emporiums dotted across the city, most of them damaged beyond recognition. But there was only one emporium I knew of in the canals, if that's where we were headed. It was the same one where Bender had salvaged his brightly colored pleasure toys.

The last I'd seen it, it'd been in disrepair, but in better shape than most. The building was sound enough, if I remembered correctly. It was in a remote part of the canals, near open water. "Any particular reason we're heading to an emporium?" I asked, knowing Dill couldn't help but brag and end up telling me everything.

"Not an emporium. *The* Emporium. That's where Hutch and Slim are. Tandor didn't have the vision, but we do. We're going to revive the pleasure industry." His tone was beyond boastful—it carried amazement. Like he couldn't believe his luck.

"The pleasure industry, huh?" I hadn't expected that.

"Yep. We're going to gather up all the seekers in the city, turn them into slaves, along with anyone else who doesn't go along with the plan. Then we're going to fix up that place and make a fortune."

A fortune of *what?*

I cleared my throat. "Um…as of the last, I don't know, maybe sixty years, give or take, most of your potential clients don't have any coin to their names. If you aren't familiar, the government gives us the meager things we need, like it always has, and folks don't have funds to spend." I was stating the obvious, but I felt it needed to be said out loud, because, you know, Hutch's master plan had some gaping flaws.

Honestly, if anyone had any funds, they'd spend it on survival, not pleasure. Well, everyone except the Dillweeds of the world.

Dill jammed the barrel of his gun farther into my shoulder, dismissing my argument with an arc of spittle that sprayed across my neck. Gross. "All that's going to change once Hutch takes charge of the city. We're going to make people *work* for their fair share, reinstate coin, and they're *all* going to spend it on pleasure." He was irritatingly smug, as if he'd masterminded the entire plan himself.

Fat fucking chance.

"What jobs are people going to do?" Now I was really curious.

"They'll clean this shitty place up."

"Where's the government going to get the coin to pay people?" I asked. "The Flotilla took most of the physical funds with them when they left." Why was anyone's guess. Who needed physical funds at sea? The Flotilla was shrouded in mystery.

"We'll make new stuff."

Dill had a dipshit answer for everything.

"Like cut some coin-looking objects out of some carbon sheeting?" I suggested helpfully.

"Yeah, maybe."

"I'm sure that'll work great." My voice held enough sarcasm that an inanimate object could have figured out my meaning.

Dill remained as obtuse as ever. "It will. Too bad you won't be around to see it. We're going to be rich."

"So," I said, just to pass the time, "what are you going to spend all your newly minted coin on?"

He didn't hesitate. "Weapons, a sweet new place to live, new clothes, and as much pleasure as I can."

Was this guy for real?

"How exactly is all that going to work? Where are you getting these new weapons?" There hadn't been any manufacturing facilities anywhere for the past thirty years. No new crafts, no new gadgets, and certainly no new guns. Dill was implying—ridiculously and somewhat delusionally—that industry was going to magically restart with nothing but sex to fuel it. Not only was it *not* going to appear, mystically rising up out of the iron-soaked puddles, but there wasn't going to suddenly be a stack of weapons that he could peruse at his leisure either. No matter how much made-up coin he'd unfairly earned.

"The slaves are going to do it." He'd uttered the words in an exasperated tone, like *I* was the moron.

"Slaves are going to start making weapons?" I should've added, *you fucking doofus.* But the gun rocking into my shoulder blade was getting uncomfortable, and I was still trying to breathe under the shirt from hell. But I had to admit that having this conversation was the best distraction I could've hoped for. I felt like I was on one of those ancient entertainment shows I'd read about, where people did silly things to get a laugh. At the time, it'd been hard to fathom such a concept, but suddenly it all made sense.

"Yeah. And other stuff." He sounded a little unsure this time, and I barely refrained from laughing.

"Man, I really wish I was going to be around to see it," I said. "That would be something else."

The craft began to drop altitude, the pilot still silent. "Shut up," Dill snapped. "I'm done with you talking." He addressed the pilot. "Land on the roof. Right over there."

The S3 settled onto its target smoothly. Before they'd blindfolded me, I'd seen the make and model of the dronecraft. These had been made for comfort. It was the first craft I'd ever been inside that my legs actually had enough room to move. I was sorry I had to exit, but not at all sorry to lose the putrid face mask.

There was a lot of hustling and hands tugging me all over. "Can somebody please take this thing off?" My voice treaded into a whine. "If you don't, you're not going to get the pleasure of killing me, because I'll already be dead by asphyxiation. And while we're at it, who cares if I see where we are? By all accounts, I'm not leaving this place alive." Clearly, none of these guys were trained in the art of kidnapping, or much of anything else, for that matter.

Someone finally obliged.

The rancid shirt was ripped free, and my nostrils widened, drawing in semi fresh air. I tilted my head up to the sky and took a deep breath, not caring if iron-laden drizzle fell right into my mouth. Once I recovered, I said, "Thank you. That was very kind." Three guys stood in front of me. They turned and began to walk me across the roof toward a makeshift entrance. My hands were still bound in front. I didn't see Dill, so I glanced over my shoulder. I took in a sharp breath.

Seven was parked next to another craft nearby.

Fuck.

They must've gotten Case, too. I knew I should've dropped him closer to Port Station. That was going to make things more complicated.

Dill popped into my line of sight, strolling out from behind the craft we'd just exited and smirking. "That's right, honey." He spread his arms wide. "Drink it all in. This is the last time you'll ever see the outdoors again. Hutch's got big plans for you, and they're going to take place right inside that Emporium. It's going to be your brand-new forever home. I heard you needed one, since the other one came to an unexpected…*end*." He snorted with braying laughter.

I was momentarily confused. "I thought the plan was to kill me. Remember, I'm in the way of your dastardly plans, and I'm not going to live long enough to see you spend all your new, hard-earned coin?"

He grumbled as a guy in front of us keyed open a door with a lime-green laser key. "If I have any say, you'd die a slow, tortured death. But Hutch wants to see how you'd be as a slave. You're going to be his shiny new toy." His face brightened as he thought about my new position in life. "I'm sure it will be entertaining, at least for a while. All the slaves are going to be wearing skimpy outfits and shaking their asses."

That sounded…revolting. "I'm no one's *toy*."

"Like you have anything to say about it." They shuffled me inside, hands prodding me down four flights of stairs. At the bottom, there was a beefy-looking guy standing in front of a honeycombed graphene door, which had obviously been set in place as a reinforcement. Dill asserted his power, pushing himself to the front of the group, snidely ordering the guard, "Step aside. I have the girl."

The guy barely acknowledged Dill as he opened the door. I was maneuvered into a surprisingly clean space. Walls had been repaired, garbage and debris nowhere in sight. It was odd to see something this put together that wasn't a government-sanctioned space— not that government areas were super nice, but they were a lot better than what the average person could accomplish on their own.

They led me through a few corridors that eventually opened into a large room. This had been the main gathering area for patrons visiting the Pleasure Emporium long ago. I knew because I'd been here once before on a salvage run. It'd been in shambles then.

But now it was clear of debris, and there were casual seating areas arranged in a few places, along with some desks along the back wall.

What was most surprising was the big Bliss Corp sign, which was made of cut metal. It had been repaired and hung on the wall. The letters glimmered with a metallic-gold sheen, reflecting the low lighting set up around the room.

It almost resembled a regular operation back in the day, if you ignored all the dents in the walls, the missing glass, broken fixtures, and the things they couldn't possibly repair because there was nothing to repair them with. A cluster of men sat together in one of the far areas.

As we came in, some of them stood, surprise etched on their faces. But for the most part, it seemed, they'd known I was coming. Dill had sounded the alarm.

A fairly tall and extremely emaciated man came forward. His cheeks were so hollow, it looked as if his tongue would get tangled up in them on a regular basis with no room to move.

That had to be Slim.

If it wasn't, this guy should be jealous of whoever got the moniker that should be rightfully his. He got in my face. "Where are my formulas, bitch?"

I didn't flinch. These guys were extremely predictable. "It's not my fault you were had by a twelve-year-old," I shot back. "And do you honestly think I'd keep valuable information like that on me? What is up with you guys?"

His face clouded. He drew an arm back like he was going to punch me. But before he could carry out his move, a voice ordered, "Stop."

Very slowly, another figure rose from the couch. "I can't have you damaging the goods. Especially when they arrived in such a pretty package." His voice was low and masculine, with an exaggerated amount of syrupy sweet. "We don't know how seekers heal from trauma they receive *before* they're injected. We know they don't do well after, so we can only assume that if she's marred now, she will stay that way."

The man moving toward me was sleek. He had that going for him.

He was taller than average, with a mane of long dark hair that floated away from his face in an arc that seemed to defy gravity. His eyes were piercing and crystal clear, a kind of light blue that I'd never seen before. They made him look like a ghost. He wore custom clothes like mine. He had what Tandor had been missing, and this guy Slim—confidence.

The only thing marring his otherwise perfect visage was a long scar, which ran from his right temple all the way down to his jaw. At least Daze had gotten that part right. He'd told me that Hutch was ugly and Slim was regular, which just proved the kid thought every adult looked the same. He was going to need some training.

Hutch reached out like he was going to brush his knuckles against my cheek. I bobbed my head out of the way and gritted my teeth. "If you touch me, you die," I snarled. He dropped his hand, and I shrugged. "Well, you're going to die anyway, but you'll just die harder and in a more painful way if you touch me."

"Such harsh words from a prisoner." He tsked like I was a child.

But he'd backed off. I considered that a win.

"Yep, you caught me," I said. "But I can assure you I won't be here for long." I glanced casually around the room. "And whatever you've got going on here is definitely not going to happen. But it's nice to see the place all spruced up. I just lost my residence." I met his ghostly gaze with a searing look of my own. "Maybe you've heard? I think I'll commandeer this space when you're gone. It's only fair, and you kind of owe me."

A slow grin spread across his face. "I heard you had a hard edge. I'm glad they weren't exaggerating. It will make things interesting." He stepped back, sweeping his arm out behind him. "I think you might be familiar with my associate? This is Case. He has no need for a surname. In fact, I'm told Case is a nickname for suit*case*, which is all he had on him when his dear old sustainers took him in."

Associate?

I tried not to gape. I really did.

Case sat behind him, not bothering to stand. He reclined there, looking at ease with all these assholes. He didn't even bother to hide it.

A loud snicker sounded behind me. "That was the best part!" Dill shrieked. "How did you not know you had an enemy in your bed all along?"

Furious didn't come close.

Red rage threatened to overtake me.

I fought to gather myself, inhaling a few needed breaths. It was only fair after getting that kind of news. "He was *never* in my bed," I bit out.

Case's facial expression didn't change as his eyes met mine.

Hutch clucked his tongue as he swung himself back toward me, his hands clapping together like he'd finalized a merger of some kind. "What a shame. Opportunities, it seems, were lost." Then his face went dark. "You want to know how it felt to be had by a twelve-year-old? How did it feel to have the man sitting next to you in your craft detonate your residence right in front of your fucking eyes?" Hutch's expression churned. I spotted rage and anger and, in the empty place where his soul should've been, desperation.

He was dangerous.

A barrage of old memories assaulted me without my permission, one after another. My eight-year-old self face-to-face with the man in charge of my demise, of ruining me, of committing acts so heinous there had been no words in my young vocabulary to describe them. He resembled the man in front of me—not physically, but the look in his eyes. They were dead. Soulless. Empty. This was a man capable of great harm, one who felt nothing when he extinguished the life of another.

I shrugged.

Then I leaned to the side, making sure I had Case's full attention. "When this is over, I'm taking the barracks, too. Just so we're clear." Turning back to Hutch, I made my expression as bland as possible. "So how are we going to do this? I don't have what you need on my person. In order to get it, you're going to have to let me go. We can arrange a swap at your earliest convenience."

Instead of getting down to the business of negotiating, Hutch grabbed my arm painfully and wheeled me around, shoving me in front of him. "Business is such a boring topic. How about we go have a look inside the Emporium? We've made so many improvements already. I think you'll enjoy what you see."

He prodded me forward, and I had no choice but to go. "Yeah, I bet."

Chapter 21

Hutch shepherded me into a long hallway that once upon a time might've held a set of massive double doors, probably made of glass, likely with the Bliss Corp logo etched on them in flowing script. Maybe the incoming patron, once through those doors, had been greeted by a hologram of a beautifully augmented woman welcoming them with a beckoning finger, flirting with them about what was to come as she led them toward their destination.

Soft, seductive music might've played from hundreds of integrated speakers, pheromones likely wafting through vents to titillate and excite. Too bad it didn't exist, because that would've been a much more enjoyable experience compared to the one that was in store for me now in this broken-down piece-of-shit building.

In its prime, it'd probably been elegantly appointed—with some of the richest fabrics and decor available in the world—because a multitrillion-dollar industry didn't skimp. The floor beneath our feet held no remnants of anything marking it as grand. Hutch's men had cleared the crap away, but the years of corrosion and degradation couldn't be erased. It looked dead.

"What do you think so far?" Hutch asked with unmasked pride, a firm grip on my elbow. Several of his men followed, but I wasn't about to look behind me to see who they were.

"I think you're insane," I answered bluntly.

He tossed his head back, his mane of hair swaying with each intake of breath as he laughed. It was a full-throated sound of pleasure. And phony as hell. I knew his anger boiled right beneath the surface. It would rear its ugly head soon enough.

The flowing-hair thing was strange and unusual. Because most of us wore our protective headgear the majority of the time, when the helmets came off, the average head of hair was a hot, tangled mess, as mine was at the moment. Not many people had time to hole up at a Pleasure Emporium, planning their evil government overthrow while keeping their hair shiny and clean.

"Wait until you see this." His voice was animated as he moved to open a door to our left.

"I'm fairly certain nothing you have in here will impress me." I received a snort in response.

The room was dimly lit. A red glow encompassed us as we moved over the threshold. I didn't have my chromes, which were in my vest, currently residing on Dill's body, or my visor, so I had to squint to make out the shapes. It was a fairly large space. A raised platform took up most of one corner.

Hutch stubbornly maneuvered me farther into the room, my feet doing their best to resist, my movements chunky and wooden.

Surprised, I made out the form of a human on top of the platform, which I now realized was a bed.

All of a sudden, the figure sat up, screeching and growling, fists opening and recurling, arms and legs tethered in place with little room to move, head shaking from side to side.

"You have a seeker chained up here?" I turned to him.

"I prefer to call them *givers*. They are equipped to *give* ultimate pleasure."

The woman thrashed, trying to free herself from her bindings. "More like *takers*. This woman looks like she would rip your dick off if you put it anywhere near her." She began moaning, the words *plush* and *need* bubbling out. "Not exactly very forthright thinking to have someone capable of harming your most sensitive parts in bed with you."

He glared at me, then held his hand up and snapped his fingers. "Bring me a dart." After one of his henchmen handed him a small dart like the one I'd seen Dill use on the seeker he called Mary, Hutch walked purposely over to the woman, who was wearing next to nothing, a couple of thin undergarments barely covering her body, and plunged the dart into her neck.

I grimaced at the squishy sound it made.

Instantly, the seeker calmed, her body going limp. A few seconds later, she began to moan, but this time her words were different. I heard *like it* and *more*. Very slowly, she started undulating. Her hips rose off the bed, her fingers raking the blankets around her, her sounds becoming more punctuated and breathy.

Hutch turned to me, his head inclined toward the woman, like I was supposed to be impressed with her abrupt turnaround from a woman who would rip a dick off to a drug-addled seductress.

I didn't care about that. I cared about what was in that dart. "Did you give her a cure?" I asked, my eyes continuing to track her movements, which were becoming more pronounced. "Doesn't look like it to me."

He gave an exasperated sigh. "A full dose might give her some relief, but we've found that a half dose creates this state." His wrist unfurled toward the woman, like he was unveiling a prize. All that was left unsaid was *ta-da.*

"The state of I'll-kill-you-in-about-an-hour? Just stick around until I shake this crap and get back to my seeker ways?"

His eyes went dark. "No, the state of arousal."

I tilted my head as I examined the poor woman, who was still undulating, her moans beginning to sound pained. "That's arousal? Huh. It looks more like she has a bowel obstruction she's trying to shake loose before she explodes." I glanced around. "Is there a waste room nearby? Maybe we can help her relieve herself."

Hutch grabbed me and spun me around.

That was getting old.

A crowd had gathered by the door. Once they saw the look in their leader's eyes, they quickly dispersed. Once it was clear, he dragged me through. We were barely two steps out before he burst through another door and tossed me in, causing me to crash to my knees.

"This is your room." His tone was steely as he stomped over to a wall and began to pluck things off. It was pretty impressive that items had been mounted there in the first place. These guys had a keen eye for getting the Pleasure Emporium ready for business. Clutching something in his fist, he stalked toward me. "Get up. See these?" He held out his hands. "We have working VR goggles and nodules. We have holograms and sensory nodes. For the first time in over sixty years, we can give a customer the complete erotic experience."

I got to my feet, which was tricky since my hands were still bound in front of me. I was thoroughly puzzled. "You're going to have to help me out here," I told him. "I thought your end game was overthrowing the government and ruling this tiny, crappy broken mess of a city. How'd you manage to downgrade to sex slavery so quickly? Did my putting an end to Tandor's life change your course?"

His big reveal into this new, twisted world wasn't having the desired effect on me, and Hutch was getting visibly agitated. A tic formed in the crease of his forehead. He clutched a pair of VR goggles in one hand and what I assumed were the nodules in the other. I'd never seen a pair, but the nodules had wires and little clampy things at the ends, so that must be what connected to your sensitive parts to provide the appropriate stimulation in conjunction with what the viewer was seeing. Looked painful to me. With gritted teeth and shaking limbs, he answered, "This is how we take down the government."

"You're going to sex them to death?"

"Once we open our doors, they will come to us. One by one. We either kill them or make them our slaves. In the end, the city will be ours."

I was going to have to revise my first impression. The man was confident, but the masterminding intelligence wasn't there. I refrained from laughing outright, but it was close. "And if they don't choose to come here for a sex-slavey adventure?"

Claire was a government worker, and she would never consider visiting a place like this, even if she hadn't heard the rumors of people missing and all-around death and destruction, which she would've.

Everyone would've.

Word about this group was already spreading. People talked. Hell, Dill had already told the first person he saw—me. This would be no secret operation.

Hutch was completely delusional if he thought this plan would work.

He stalked forward, his face menacing, the tic now a full-blown twitch. It made his eyebrow jump. His black hair bounced above his shoulders. It would've been mesmerizing if the situation hadn't been so painfully nauseating. "No need to worry yourself with the details," he cooed. "A plan is in place, and it will work beautifully."

I scanned the room. It was set up nearly identical to the last one, with a platform bed in the corner. I guessed that's where all the action would take place. On one of the walls, the remnants of an integrated screen were still visible. No doubt for broadcasting explicit scenes. I glanced at the door.

Like the other room, an assemblage of people had gathered. I yawned. I would've lifted my arms to stretch if they hadn't been cuffed in front of me. "I'm going to need a nap pretty soon."

Hutch hauled me to his chest by the arm, tossing the coveted VR goggles and nodules at someone as we passed. "The last thing you're going to be doing is sleeping."

He dragged me back into the main room, the contingency following like brainless children. The only one who hadn't joined in the procession, Case, hadn't even bothered to get up. He sat in the same position, legs crossed, a bland expression on his face, his fingertips drumming against the arm of the chair.

Disgust bubbled in my throat.

It was hard to admit that I'd actually begun to trust him. The seeds had been sown—almost without my permission—and trust had begun to sprout. Lucky for me, those seedlings could be dug up and tossed out a scraper window just as easily. "Too busy to join our little tour, asshole?" I spat as Hutch forced me into a seat across from him, pressing my shoulders down with force. I sat with a thump.

Case shrugged. "I've seen it already."

"I'm sure you have. Did you help with all the cleaning and sweeping? Or possibly loaned them a sledge so they could arrange everything just so on the walls?"

He sat up abruptly, his elbows braced on his thighs, the skin around his eyes tight. "We all do what we have to do to survive."

My gut roiled in disgust. I'd let this guy get close to me. "What did they offer you in exchange for your soul?" I jerked forward in my seat only to be shoved backward. "Whatever it was, I hope it rots you from the inside out."

Hutch walked around my chair, followed by Dill, who was smirking. It was the only expression he knew how to make. "Such passion," Hutch said, turning to address Case. "See, I told you. She will be our main draw. No one will be able to stay away once they know we have her." He reached inside his jacket and pulled out a dart, this one slightly bigger than the one he had just used on the seeker. "Once she's injected, we will monitor her closely. If you like"—he inclined his head toward Case—"you can taste her first."

Dill interrupted, "Hey, you said whoever brought her in got her first! That's me." He slapped an open palm against his chest. Then he began to cough. Through his racking hacks, he managed, "If you go back on your word"—*cough, cough*—"everybody's going to think you're full of shit." He coughed again, spittle catching on his chin.

Hutch asked, "Is that blood?"

Dill halfheartedly swiped at his face. "I don't know." He brought his hand in front of his face. His eyes widened. "Why the fuck am I bleeding?" He coughed so hard he had to bend over. On the way up, more blood, mixed with spittle, dribbled down his neck. His eyes met mine, and he lunged toward me. "You did this to me, didn't you?"

My face remained impassive as I leaned forward slowly. "To be fair," I said, "I did tell you that if you took my vest, you'd die. Did you think I was joking?" My bottom lip popped out as I made a sad face. "That's really too bad, Dill. I rarely make jokes when it comes to death and dying. I was actually pretty impressed with myself for giving you a warning in the first place. It was kind of like a test"—I dropped my voice to a whisper—"which it seems you failed big-time."

He bared his teeth, which were now a dark scarlet, as Hutch's men held him back. I crossed my legs and sat back. "I wouldn't get too close to him, fellas. That's the funny thing about radium balls. They're not too choosy about who they infect."

Two of the guys immediately dropped their hands and backed away.

Hutch's voice was feral as he addressed Dill. "Did you check the pockets before you put that thing on?"

Dill's shocked expression was comical. Apparently, he was capable of making more than one face. "Well…I…" He jabbed a hand in my direction. "She did. She emptied them before she gave it to me."

"It seems she didn't, you moron," Hutch hissed. "Take him out of here. Put him in a containment room and don't go near it for the next forty-eight hours."

"It might take a wee bit longer than that." I brought up my cuffed wrists, pinching my thumb and index finger together. "The radium contained in that stone has a density of over one million units per gig. In forty-eight hours, he will be fairly charred, but the radium will be happy and active for far longer." I was going to miss that vest.

The retreating men were forced to take a hands-on approach with Dill, who was struggling like a madman. "Bitch! You bitch!" he screamed as they dragged him away. "I'll kill you for this!"

"Escort him out of the building," Hutch called after them. "I don't care what you do with him, as long as he's contained." Within seconds, Hutch reached down and yanked me out of my seat, hoisting me to his chest, his eyes wild and dark. "Do you think this is a game?" I smirked, and he shook me. "You're about to become my slave, and once you're infected, you won't be able to wreak any more havoc. I doubt you'll be laughing then."

"Isn't everything just one big game?" I deadpanned. "Each of us making our calculated moves until our enemies die? And, just so you know, it's about to get increasingly more hilarious, right NOW!"

Chapter 22

I kneed Hutch in the groin with more than enough force to make it hurt. Very satisfyingly, and with a whoosh of exhaled breath, he went down, crumpling like a champ, howling in pain.

At the same time, the door we'd originally come through from the roof blew inward, like I'd known it would.

Lockland and Bender entered, their weapons up.

Not only had I activated the radium ball before giving the vest to Dill—the outer shell took an hour to corrode, which I'd been fairly certain about, but not absolutely—but I'd also locked the tech phone on and muted it before Dill had swiped it out of my hands. There was a lot I could do inside my pockets.

My crew had heard everything from that moment forward.

Hutch continued to howl as Lockland and Bender began to fire on the remaining men. Surprisingly, I also heard shots out in the corridor, where they'd taken Dill. I turned, just in time to watch Daze scamper through the entrance carrying a laser gun almost as big as my Gem in shaky hands.

I called, "Easy there, Daze—"

Before I could finish, I was yanked to the ground, Hutch's breath in my ear. I'd been so focused on Daze, I hadn't been paying attention. "Even if you manage to eliminate us all," he panted, "you are still going to pay the price." His words were shaky and broken and filled with pain. His fists were like a pair of vises as they clutched me around the waist.

Satisfaction at his pain welled in my chest, even though I was pissed I hadn't taken him out completely before he'd regained his strength.

"Let her go!" Daze charged us, the too-big-for-him weapon bobbing up and down as he ran.

I tried to respond, but Hutch clamped a hand over my mouth and rolled us over. I felt the needle prick my neck the instant before he announced, "Stop, or I infect her."

Daze was too emotional to think straight. He kept right on coming until a figure stepped in his way, causing him to pull up short.

Case brought his pulse gun up, aiming it at Hutch and me, and said, "Daze, go sit down," he ordered the kid. "Do it, or she dies."

"See that?" Hutch chuckled as he hauled me up off the ground. "You can't kill us all."

I couldn't speak, because Hutch's hand was still

tightly pressed to my lips, the needle sliding in and out of my skin as we moved.

Daze seemed unsure what to do.

Behind them, Lockland and Bender were still engaged with the others. More men had run through another doorway. But I had no fear of them losing this battle. It would take only a few more moments.

Case's voice was like ice as he said to Daze, "Go. Sit. Down."

I began to struggle, causing the needle to scratch along my neck, drawing blood. Rivulets dripped down my neck. I didn't want Daze to sit down. I wanted him to get the hell out of here. This was no place for a kid.

Plus, I didn't want him to watch me die.

Before I could make my displeasure known in a much more concrete way, Darby barreled through the doorway, skidding to a stop once he saw me.

The pure, unadulterated look of confusion on his face said it all. He immediately rushed forward and grabbed Daze, steering him away, reading the look on my face accurately.

"If anybody moves, she dies," Case announced to the room as he leveled his gun at my head, his finger engaging the trigger.

My eyes darted around. Lockland and Bender had finished. Bodies were strewn around the room. They could each take Case out, but if he let go of the trigger, it would be over for me.

They stood a few meters behind him, both of their faces set.

More people were going to die in this room before this was over. I just hoped it wouldn't be me or my crew.

"We've regained the upper hand," Hutch said to Case, panting. "We have the girl. We can take care of these guys. They won't do anything to harm her. Then we infect her and resume our business. We can get more recruits on board. People in this city cave easily." He was delusional if he thought he would win a battle against my crew. He'd basically just told them he was going to make me a Plushie.

"You can't infect her," Case said, his tone eerily calm.

"Oh, I think I can." Hutch plunged the dart farther into my neck. All it would take now was for him to depress the button on top, where I knew his thumb was hovering.

"What I mean is you can't do it here. Once she's injected, her crew will take us both out."

Bender grunted an affirmative.

It was only a matter of time. Case and Hutch were outmatched, and Case knew it.

Hutch shook his head. "I infect her, then we take them out." The tenseness of his tone was clear. He was grasping for anything.

"No," Case said. "The only way we're going to get out of here alive is if you let her go."

"As soon as I let her go, we're dead," Hutch snarled. "She's the only thing we have."

"I said let her go." Case slid his gun a few centimeters to the right, finding a new target.

Hutch's rage took a physical form. He quaked with it. "It seems you found a taste for her after all." He'd uttered the words like bile had coated his throat. "I can't let that happen."

"Let her go."

"I'm a dead man anyway. Why shouldn't I end it with a little fun?"

"If you release her," Case said, "you can walk out of here. You have my word."

Hutch snorted. "Your word? I don't think so."

The dart plunged deeply into my neck, searing liquid shooting into my bloodstream.

I tried to get away, arching forward, my brain racing with the implications. The fucker had just given me a dose of Plush.

Case's bullet entered Hutch's forehead a moment after the bastard jammed the button down. Hutch collapsed to the ground as his body began to liquefy.

The sounds around me became muted as the blood in my ears pounded like an unforgiving drum. I stumbled forward, falling to my knees, my palms hitting the floor. My nerve endings were on fire, tingling like I'd been electrocuted. My fingertips didn't even feel like they were attached to my body. I wanted to retch, but nothing came up.

Someone lifted me off the ground.

Muted voices erupted around me. "Get her into one of the rooms." I think it was Lockland. His voice was beautiful. How come I'd never noticed that before? It was attached to vibrant colors like green and orange.

The colors erupted like starbursts behind my eyes. It made me smile. Lockland was nice. He'd been like a second father to me.

"I have the pico," Darby said. His tone quaked, but it was warm and pink. It made me want to hug him. I tried to reach out, my arms extending, my back bending. I couldn't find him. It made me sad.

A voice in my ear commanded, "Stay still." Everything exploded blue, like a blast from a bomb. The color of the sea in my dreams rippled through me, igniting something deep within. I tried to open my eyes to see who had spoken, but my eyelids were too heavy.

Why couldn't I open them?

My hands groped in front of me, bound by something. Warmth flooded through me as I tried to reach out and touch the blue. "She's losing control," the same voice said. "I won't be able to hold her for very much longer."

"Set her here."

The arms cradling me laid me down.

I was alone…I didn't want to be alone. It was so cold. I wanted to be warm. I cried out. The blue words were magnetic. I wanted to hear them again. So many sensations. I reached out with my fists. This time, I wouldn't let it go.

"The drug works in stages." Darby's voice penetrated my desires, grabbing my attention. Why was Darby here? Where was I? Everything was so beautiful. I just wanted to let go. If I let go, I could feel all the colors, let them run free. "We need to get whatever they were using to calm the seekers into her before she reaches the final stage. Can you move so I can see her pupils?"

"She has a death grip on my arm," the blue voice said, stroking my mind, enticing me with possibilities.

"Then just check yourself. Are her pupils dilated?"

"I can't tell, they're closed."

A few moments later, rustling sounded in my ear, and the warmth tried to escape. "Holly, Hol, I need you to open your eyes," Darby called. His pink tone was pleasant, but not nearly as intense as the blue one. "Can you hear my voice? The data says if you focus hard enough, you can."

"That asshole gave her a full syringe." Bender, I knew Bender. His voice was scarlet mixed with ice. Hot and cold. He was strong, he could save me! He'd done it before. "Was it a single dose or more?"

I clawed myself back to the surface, past all the colors, through the tingling, locked on Bender's voice. I licked my lips, my hips rolling as I spoke. "Can't… want…more…"

"That's okay, just open your eyes for me," Darby coaxed.

It took everything I had to do as he asked. I couldn't focus. Only the feelings undulating inside me were crystal clear. They needed a release. "Want… out…"

"I know," Darby murmured, patting my shoulder. "We're going to get you there. I promise."

Another wave of nerve-ending explosions filtered through me. My eyes fluttered shut, my head lolled from side to side. The only thing that kept me from floating away forever was the warmth that I was still grasping on to. I dug my nails in.

"Is she going to be okay?" a small voice asked. "Can you cure her?" All the colors of the rainbow exploded in my mind at once. The voice was fragile and innocent. *Have to help it.* I began to thrash. *Nothing can happen to that voice. Have to protect it.*

My mind was inundated. Everything was intermixing, confusing me. I couldn't hold on.

"Get him out of here," the blue voice commanded. "She's reacting to him."

"Daze, I'm going to do my best to help her." Darby's pink rose to the surface. "If you want to help, go and find me some of those darts. The ones Holly said they used on that seeker. Check everyone's pockets. There has to be a few out there."

"And shoot anything that moves," Bender grumbled in red. "Use the gun the way I showed you."

My grip on the warmth tightened. *Can't be alone. Never be alone.* My reality was breaking apart, but I wanted to stay. I had to stay. Struggling, I lifted my head. "Help...me..." My voice sounded breathy in my own ears.

Far away, scared, yearning.

"Can't you do this any faster?" The blue voice was impatient, angry. I opened my eyes. When he spoke, something in me surged. I couldn't control it. It made me furious and lightheaded at the same time. My hand reached for his chest. Once I had some material in my grasp, I pulled him closer. He moved downward until I felt his hair brush my lips. The soft tingles against my mouth sent waves of something I didn't understand rushing through me.

My rage anchored me, helping me stay rooted in the here and now. "You…fucked…me over…"

"Never." His voice was firm, making the blue reverberate inside of me. I shivered, grinding my ass into the platform. My mind screamed in protest, hating every second of not being in control of my body.

This was hell, not ecstasy.

Once again, the anger allowed me to stay coherent. I gritted my teeth, spitting, "Liar!"

"Do more of that," Darby encouraged. "When she's angry, she's fighting the effects. Keep her pissed off until I can figure out what we need to add to this formula."

"It shouldn't be too hard to keep her pissed off," Bender said. "You were playing both sides, Militia. Don't think we're going to forget about it anytime soon. I don't care if you ended up killing that asshole."

When Case exhaled, I felt it spread across my cheek. My grip was like steel. I couldn't even feel my fingertips. Anger roiled deep inside, penetrating my brain.

"I wasn't playing both sides." Blue beamed forward. It was absolute. A jolt of sensation hit my inner core.

"Then why didn't you just kill them all when you

had the chance?" Lockland argued. "You were in his presence before Holly showed up."

"I was going to once I had the final piece."

"Piece of goddamn *what?*" Bender asked, his voice harsh and unbending. Fire and ice.

"The formula for the cure on the quantum drive is incomplete."

"I got it! I got it!" the small voice shrieked.

I began to thrash again, tugging Case along with me. A kaleidoscope of colors danced in my mind. Reality was dimming as the sensations took over. There was nothing I could do. I couldn't stop it.

"Quiet, kid," Bender said. "You're agitating her."

My head throbbed. The colors were building to a crescendo. They made me happy. Blissfully content. It wasn't a familiar feeling.

"Here's the dart." I had to struggle to hear the small voice. "I found it in that guy's pocket. It was disgusting. Slimy stuff was oozing out of his eyes and mouth and everything."

Daze.

The name floated in the space of my mind, the letters all spelled out, followed by an image of him. Smiling, tousled hair, innocent, forgiving eyes. I rolled onto my side. He wasn't safe here. I tried to make myself see. I opened my eyes.

Darby held something in his fist. He brought it toward me. Case's hand shot out, stopping him. "No."

The blue light danced in my brain, going high, then crashing back down. Over and over again. I closed my eyes, my head rolling. The sensations beckoned me, taunting me, enticing me.

"What are you talking about?" Darby argued. I struggled to focus. "According to what I've read, it could put her into a calmer state and inhibit the drug's ability to progress."

"It doesn't do that." Case was firm. "I've seen it. The state she will go into is not one of calm." My fingertips tingled, and I groaned. "I haven't seen one seeker improved. Find a cure or nothing."

Darby sputtered, "But that could take days. Her genes could be permanently altered by then!"

Colors, tones, and textures blurred. Like a thousand starbursts going off in my mind at once. I had to let go. The colors would make me happy. I knew they would. I deserved happiness. All I had to do was give in.

"I said a cure or nothing."

Blue wavered and then exploded.

I writhed on the bed. I struggled to pull my head up, whispering, "Cure…need cure…"

"Darby." Lockland's voice was green and electric. "Can you figure it out?"

"I…think so. I've only been reading the data for a few hours. I'd need to go to the lab to do it. If I can analyze the contents of this dart, I can find out what's missing."

"It's some kind of powder," Case said.

"How do you know that?" Darby asked. Pink pulsed like a heartbeat.

Powder, powder, powder.

I wanted to laugh. It was so funny.

"Hutch had it." Blue spiraled outward. "He wouldn't share its location with anyone. Whatever supplies they had were limited at best, but the location was top secret."

"What's the powder made from?" Bender asked.

"Seaweed." Blue lashed down like a laser.

"The stuff that used to grow in the ocean?" Lockland asked. Greens and purples swirled.

Everything began to fade.

Bliss was on the other side. I wanted it. It was beautiful. I deserved it. My grip on Case's arm slackened, falling away.

"Hey, stay with us." Blue shot directly into my ear as something shook me. It danced in my mind. "I almost let you die, remember?"

I did remember. Case's smug look filtered into my muddled mind. He'd been sitting there waiting for me. How could he do that? He was a traitor. He couldn't be trusted. I growled, "Bastard…*hate* you…"

"Good." Blue pierced me, making me shiver and moan.

"Sodium alginate." The sound of Darby's fingers on the keyboard tapped out blasts of light in my mind. "Of course. It's a compound that binds drug remnants together and prevents them from being absorbed by the body. We have to find that powder."

I let go. There was nothing for me here.

Chapter 23

"Holly? Can you hear me?" Darby's voice sounded like it was at the end of a tunnel, far, far away. Hands prodded me. "Hol, it's time to wake up."

I groaned.

Just let me sleep, dammit. I tried to roll over.

"Wake the hell up," Bender growled. "Enough already."

"Give her more." The tone was firm. Case. What was he doing here? He'd betrayed us.

Oh, wait.

I kind of remembered. It was hazy. There had been a lot of colors.

"I've already given her more than the data states," Darby sputtered. "There's no precedent for this. We don't know what it's going to do to her."

"We can see what it's doing. It's curing her."

My brain was at war with my body, urging me to wake up. I was getting angry. I just wanted to sleep.

Something pricked my arm. "*Ow*! What the hell, Darby?" The words tumbled out of my mouth before I knew what I was saying.

My brain had won.

Laughter sounded. "Best back up," Bender warned. "She's about to come to, and when she does, she's going to be pissed the fuck off."

My vision swam as my mind tried to make sense of what was happening. Everything felt heavy: my head, my arms, my legs.

I squinted. The first thing I focused on were two innocent eyeballs less than a meter from my face. They were wide and full of fear. "Hey, kid." My voice broke at the end, unused to uttering words. "Can you get me a drink of water?" I watched as a smile spread across his small features, a toothy grin replacing the uncertainty.

Slowly, my vision cleared. We were still at the Emporium, in the room, ironically, that Hutch had called mine.

"She's awake! She's awake!" Daze danced away from me, turning in a circle before hurrying back to my side. "Darby didn't know if he could do it, but I did." His words rushed out. "I knew he could. And guess who found the powder? Guess, guess!"

"My coin is on you, kid." I tried to turn over and groaned with the effort as my body reluctantly obeyed my commands. "Now how about that water?"

Lockland appeared in front of me, holding a cup. "How do you feel?" he asked, handing me the wonderful, life-giving liquid.

"Like I crashed my craft into a graphene wall without a fucking harness on." I struggled up on an elbow and took the water, bringing it to my lips, downing it in a single swallow. I handed the cup back to Lockland. "More."

He left, and Bender and Darby came into view. Darby's face hovered above mine as he inspected me, his fingers poking and prodding. "You scared us, Hol. I wasn't sure you would come back."

I ran a hand over my face, draping my arm over my eyes like a blanket. The room was too bright. "How long have I been out?" My mouth was still dry, my head pounding.

Overall, I felt like a steaming pile of shit.

"Almost thirty hours. I'm sorry it took so long. I had to analyze the contents in the dart, and my lab is not fully stocked. But if it wasn't for Daze, you wouldn't be here. He found the secret ingredient."

I moved my arm as Lockland came back, but before he could hand me the water, Daze took the cup. "Here's more water." The kid's face was endearing as he set it into my open palm.

When I was done drinking, I set the cup next to my head and tried to sit up. Then thought better of it and stayed put. "Nice going, Daze." I turned to glance at him. His whole face was one big smile.

"It was easy," he began to jabber. "I just had to think like a bad guy would think."

"Is that so?" I murmured. "And how do bad guys think?"

"Well," Daze continued, "they're not exactly smart like you, or…or Lockland or Bender. If somebody like you hid it, it would be tricky to find. But for a bad guy, they just look for the easiest place they can guard."

"It sounds like you figured it out," I said. "That's the same way you salvage for stuff." It was time to come back to the here and now. I braced my arms on the platform and struggled to sit up. Darby tried to help me, but I shook my head. "Let me do it." Once I was up, I met Bender's gaze. "Please tell me somebody took care of Dill. If not, we're all going to be radioactive pretty soon."

He gave a short nod. "We made a couple of the guys take him out of here. Locked them all in a few blocks away."

Lockland leaned against the platform bed, crossing his arms. "I didn't know you had access to a radium ball. Those things are lethal. Before the dark days, they were for government use only, highest access. They're super concentrated, the ultimate form of chemical warfare."

"Yeah," I said as I massaged my face. I still felt like hell. "I know. I found it a few years ago. It took me a while to figure out what it was. I was lucky I didn't set the damn thing off myself. I knew one day it would come in handy. I guess I chose the right day."

"How did you get it on him?" Lockland asked.

"The asshole was easy to play. He wanted my vest. I reached in and activated it before he took it. Then I baited him to put it on." I swung my legs over the side.

Suddenly, I remembered something and shot Darby a questioning glance. "Tell me you gave the cure for that woman in the next room. The seeker who was bound to the bed?"

He nodded, sheepishly glancing down at his feet. "I actually tried it on her first. I didn't...I didn't...want to kill you."

"And?" I knew what I wanted him to say.

"Well, she's not doing as well as you are, I'll put it that way. But she's better, more coherent. She can understand some rudimentary things. I'm not sure how long she's been a seeker, but it's been long enough to significantly change things in her body. By my guess, she'll need quite a few more doses to come close to healing as well as you. Then we'll have to just wait and see."

"Okay, then give her the doses."

He shook his head sadly. "There aren't any more."

"What do you mean? They had all those darts." I locked my arms and jumped down. My legs weakened for a moment, but they held up. *Thanks, legs.* I leaned against the bed. Lockland was next to me, Darby in front, Daze near him. Bender stood about a meter behind, arms crossed. Case was nowhere in sight. I'd heard his voice earlier. He must've ducked out. I was fine with that.

"Actually, they were only able to make a handful before you guys took Tandor out. That's why they needed the quantum drive back. Without it, they didn't have access to the formulas," Darby said. "I went back to the lab that I'd been using with Marta. That's definitely where they'd put the serum together. Most of the ingredients were there, but they were running low on everything. The missing link that cured you was the sodium alginate. It used to be abundant before the dark days. It comes from a water plant called seaweed. The alginate prohibits absorption and binds the drug in the bloodstream so it can exit your system efficiently. Without it, they achieved the quasi-cure, the dart that made seekers—" he cleared his throat "—more coherent and…pliable." That was a nice way of putting it. "They only had enough sodium alginate to make enough for three doses. I gave you two, and Mary one."

"Is all the data you need to make more serum on the drive?" I asked.

"Not all of it. It's incomplete. According to Case," Darby said, "Tandor's father was a scientist who worked for the government. Finding a way to cure Plush addiction was his life's ambition, but he did it in seclusion, somewhere in the South. The quantum drive was his."

"And Case knew this because he was in league with them all along?" I ran my hands through my hair, but didn't get very far. My gloves were gone, as was my helmet and vest, which I would never see again. So many things to fix. But I was alive. "He was playing both sides the entire time."

"Possibly not," Lockland replied with an edge, which caused me to turn and look at him, crossing my arms, a pissy look on my face.

"Explain." This I had to hear.

"It seems they'd been pursuing him from the beginning, wanting his allegiance. He led them on just enough, so they never knew where his loyalties lay. It was pure luck that no one survived Tandor's death at the gorge and came back to tell the story. Or they'd have known Case was responsible for killing the others with his craft. Once he came back to the city, he picked up where he left off and infiltrated their inner circle. When you procured the drive, and it showed the formulas, he knew we had to get the sodium alginate powder Hutch bragged about before he could get rid of them for good."

"And you believe all that crap?" I huffed.

Lockland inclined his head about three centimeters. "He told me this tale last night in this very room when he refused to leave your side."

"So that's it? Now you trust him? Hutch told me he was responsible for blowing up my fucking residence." I pushed off from the platform and stalked away, thankful my legs kept me up, even though they shook like they were made of uncured hydrogel. "He was sitting in the main room when I arrived, all smug and pompous." I jabbed my arm into the air. "And before Hutch infected me with Plush, I confronted him. He told me he was doing whatever it took to stay alive, which I believe is the truth. He wouldn't hesitate to turn on us. I'm not ready to trust him."

"Fine, then we don't." Lockland's voice was even.

"I agree with Holly," Bender said. "We take it real

slow. He's out for himself. If Hutch had taken us out, would he have killed him? Or would he have stuck around to make some coin on the new enterprise? Hard to know."

Darby had taken a seat, ignoring our back-and-forth, the pico open on his lap. Daze stood in the middle of the room, looking a little forlorn. I went over and slung my arm across his skinny shoulders. "What do you think, kid? Do we trust the asshole or not?"

Daze inclined his head, his mouth falling open. "You really want my opinion?"

"Sure. You're one of us now. Aren't you the one who found the powder needed to save my life? By the way, you didn't finish telling me where you found it."

"It was stuck in the bottom of his boot."

"Shut up," I said. "His boot?"

He nodded his head solemnly. "He *should've* put it somewhere random, in a building someplace. If he'd done that, we never would've found it in a hundred million years. But I knew he wouldn't do that. He wasn't smart enough."

"How did you know to check in his boot?" I asked.

Bender cleared his throat on the end of a chuckle. "The kid damn near stripped him naked. When it wasn't anywhere to be seen, he started ripping apart his helmet and his boots. He was a machine." Judging by Bender's tone, the kid had impressed him. That was a hard thing to do. I was happy for Daze.

Daze reached out and tentatively grabbed my hand. "I didn't want you to die."

"And I didn't want to die, so thank you very much." I gave him a squeeze. "Now, back to Case. Do we trust the asshole or not?"

"How about asking the asshole himself?" Case stood in the doorway, an arm casually propped halfway up the jamb. He was projecting a don't-care attitude, but I noticed the tightness around his eyes, his telltale giveaway.

I settled my hands on my hips. "That's dependent on whether or not I'm even interested in talking to the asshole, which, frankly, I'm not."

Before he could respond, an anguished cry sounded from the other room.

Chapter 24

I made it to the room first, rushing over to the raised platform in the corner. I was disheartened to see the woman still restrained, but at least someone had taken the time to get her dressed.

It took me a moment, but I realized she was the seeker I'd seen in the street with Dill. Her name was Mary. I hadn't recognized her before. "It's okay," I soothed, rubbing her arm. She was delirious, her eyes closed, her head thrashing. I set the palm of my hand on her forehead, which was fiery to the touch. "We're going to help you." She seemed to calm a bit at the sound of my voice, her movements easing.

Darby came up behind me, the others gathered just behind. He laid two fingers on her wrist. "Her pulse has increased."

"What does that mean?" I asked.

"It's hard to know for sure. She's been asleep most

of the time. It could be that the effects of the cure I've given her are beginning to diminish."

"Has she ever been fully aware?"

"Not really," he said. "Although some of the words she's been moaning have been more coherent, and she's been calmer."

At the sounds of our voices, she turned her head, her eyes rapidly blinking. I leaned forward. "Mary? Is that your name?" One of her hands reached out and clawed my arm. She tried to bring the other one over, but it was tethered. Darby gripped my shoulder to try to guide me away. I shook my head. "No. I think she's trying to communicate. Let's give her a chance." I brought my hand up to her forehead once again and stroked it, smoothing her hair back. "Mary, we're going to help you. I swear. We're going to figure out a real cure and get you back to normal. It's just going to take a little time."

She stopped struggling.

I placed my hand in hers. She gripped it tightly. She stopped blinking as her breathing evened out. "Yes…my name…is Mary…"

I'd had to lean over to catch her words. "It's nice to meet you, Mary." She lay quiet, possibly asleep. After a moment, I eased my hand back, trying not to wake her. I glanced around the group. "How are we going to do this?"

"I want to help her, too." Darby nodded vigorously. "We all do. But that might be out of the question."

I steered him away from Mary's bed so we wouldn't

disturb her. Everyone followed us out to the main room. Hutch and all of his men were gone, but the aftereffects of the fight were still apparent in the form of overturned furniture and dried blood.

I turned to Darby, taking a seat on one of the chairs. "Tell us what you need. Whatever it is, I'm sure we can find it. Not only do we have to help Mary, we have to help them all."

Darby held the pico under his arm. He walked over to a table, set it down, opened it and began to type rapidly.

"I'm in," Bender said, taking a seat across from me. "Whatever you need, we'll figure it out."

"If we can do this," Lockland added, "it will change the course of our world as we know it."

"Change what as we know it?" The familiar voice came from the doorway.

I jumped out of my seat. "Claire!" I met her halfway, giving her a big hug. I was almost a meter taller than she was, but her stature more than made up for it. She was tough as titanium and had never taken any of my crap, which was why I'd gravitated toward her. I'd been nine years old at the time. She'd just turned twenty-five. I'd been missing my mother, and she'd filled that role on the occasions I'd needed it most.

I tried to pull back.

"I'm not finished yet." She embraced me for a few seconds longer, and when she was good and ready, she held me at arm's length. Her dark hair was wrapped up in a compact bun. For the first time, I noticed a few gray hairs wisping at the sides of her temples. "I heard we almost lost you, not once, but twice. That's completely unacceptable. Haven't I taught you anything?"

I gave a full-throated laugh. "Hey, I'm alive, aren't I? If you could've seen me in action, I think you would've been proud."

"I'm always proud." She gave me another smile as she moved around me, nodding around the group in greeting. "I came here to inform you of what's going on. The government is fractured. I can't stay long. They're monitoring my movements. They know I smuggled Darby out." Her eyes rested on Case. She moved forward, holding out her hand. "Are you the man who ended this Hutch person's life?"

"I am." He reached out and shook her hand, his eyes meeting mine over her head, one eyebrow rising, a *told you so* look on his face.

I snorted. "Just because she's shaking your hand doesn't mean everything is fine. Any one of us could've killed that piece of shit."

"But you didn't, I did." His voice was firm.

Before I could explain to him how wrong he was, Claire interrupted. "And who's this young man?" She stood in front of Daze.

I nodded at the kid to introduce himself. He stood ramrod straight. In Claire's presence, that was an automatic response, mostly because anyone who was paying attention knew she'd call you out for it if you weren't on your best behavior. "I'm Daze. My real name is Robert, but everyone calls me Daze. I'm

Holly's sustainee." His chin stuck out, defying her to say otherwise.

I barely contained a giggle.

Claire's expression didn't change. She was a pro. Her job in the government was to deal with street kids and help keep them alive. She bent over and held out her hand. "It's nice to meet you, Daze. You landed an excellent sustainer. Congratulations."

"Thanks." He blushed as he shook her hand.

Claire stood, back to business, turning to address us all. "I'm incredibly relieved that you've taken out this threat. It was a major one, but I'm sorry to report that there's been an infiltration inside the government. I'm just learning bits and pieces about it now. I don't know if it originated from the group you just defeated or not, but the people on the inside have been swaying attitudes and loyalties, using threats and tactics to try and convince the workers it's time for new leadership. Based on what I'm hearing, there could be an uprising at any moment."

"How can we help stop it?" I asked. An overthrow of any kind would harm this city—a city holding on by the thinnest of filaments, ready to topple once and for all. Just like Tandor and Hutch, anybody sneaking in to stir up trouble never had good intentions for the people. It would just bring more misery.

Claire took a seat and folded her hands in her lap. "I'm not sure. I'm working on it from the inside. I've amassed a small group of loyalists who are willing to fight any threat. But it's hard to stand up against something when we don't know who they are and who's calling the shots. They've been very discreet, but effective. With the dismantling of this group here, it could be the end of it. Or not. Time will tell."

"Has Lockland told you about the cure we're working on? The one for Plush?" I asked.

Her gaze snapped from me, to Lockland, to Darby, then back again. "What cure? All Lockland said was to come to this location and that you had almost died. Twice."

Lockland interjected smoothly, "I couldn't very well broadcast what was happening. We don't have any code for what's going on here." He shrugged. "So I made do."

"Is it true?" Her voice held excitement as she rose, gripping the sides of the chair. "If it is, it could change the game." She began to pace, her arms moving animatedly. "Most of the government would rally around a cure, even those who are beginning to turn in favor of the new aggressors." She scanned the room. "I say most, because there've been rumors in recent months—on top of these new allegations about infiltrators—that a top-secret government group no one has ever heard of before, called the Bureau of Truth, has been making Plush for years. This alleged group reportedly distributes the drug to all these poor addicts to keep them contained." She stopped moving, her head angling down as if her brain had to process a few things before she could continue. No one dared interrupt. When she was ready, she lifted her head and continued, "The gossip has only spread recently. So, to me, that means things are reaching a boiling point. In my nineteen years of service to the city, I've never heard a single thing about the Bureau of Truth. The rumors are that its creation started after the Flotilla departed, before my time in the government. So, until we figure out what it is they do and who is involved, we won't know what we're up against. But for the rest of the government, I can safely say that finding a way to bring people back from Plush would infuse new life into this city." Her face was a mix of excitement and relief. "If a cure happened, I'm certain we could gain the support we would need to prevent any coup. I can't believe a cure is even possible."

I shifted my gaze to Darby, who cleared his throat. "It's true," he said. "It worked on Holly, but she'd only been infected for a short time in the scope of things. In going over the formulas we found on the quantum drive, I can see they've been tampered with to omit the sodium alginate powder. That might not be the only omission. It's my feeling that whomever Tandor got this from, they either changed it because they were worried about it getting into the wrong hands, or they were purposely trying to mislead. Either way, it's incomplete. The only place I can figure it out for certain will be in the lab. But acquiring all the ingredients will be tricky at best. As far as I know, seaweed doesn't grow anymore, and that's not all I need."

"We'll get whatever—" I started.

"You were infected with Plush?" Claire moved

quickly toward me, concern straining her voice. "How did that happen?"

"I'm okay now," I assured her, grasping her outstretched hands. "I wasn't infected for long, and Hutch won't be infecting anyone else, because we took him out." Case snorted, and my eyes shot to his. "Hey, you're going to have to stop taking credit for something we all could've—"

"He's the only one who could've killed him," Daze interrupted, surprising me. "Well, without all of us dying, too."

"What are you talking about?" I asked, dropping Claire's hands as we both turned toward the kid.

Daze glanced at Case and then back at me. "If anyone else would've shot him with any other gun, he would've exploded."

"How could you possibly know that?" Bender asked, his disbelief talking for the rest of us.

Daze shrugged, idly kicking something on the ground. "When I took off his clothes to look for the powder, he was wired. I think he was hoping you would use a laser or something on him. The wires were connected to some hydro-bombs stuffed in his pockets." Daze lifted his head. "Lockland took care of it."

I turned to Lockland, my expression accusing. "Why didn't you say anything?"

His face remained impassive. "We trust him when you trust him. There was nothing to say." He was referring to Case and that it didn't matter if he'd known he was the only one who could've killed Hutch.

Claire cleared her throat. "Honestly, does it really matter who killed whom? The important thing is that he's gone and you're fine." She took my hand again. "Do you remember how it felt?"

"Bits and pieces," I replied. "I remember feeling strange. There were a lot of colors and weird things lighting up in my mind. I definitely craved pleasure. My body demanded it. That stuff is incredibly potent."

Bender coughed into his fist. "You tried to disrobe a number of times."

"You kept calling out a name," Lockland said, his voice breaking into laughter.

"Case was very patient," Bender added as the two of them guffawed.

"Very fucking funny." I scowled. "I could've died, and you two are acting like a couple of teenage assholes. In *case* you've forgotten, I was given a very powerful hallucinogenic drug that messed with my mind. None of my actions were conscious on my part."

"Disrobing wasn't the only thing you wanted to do—"

I walked over and held my fist in front of Bender's face, my expression like ice. "I will not be held accountable for things I did under the influence of a drug that drives people out of their goddamned minds and modifies their DNA. Are we clear?" I turned to give Lockland the same hard stare. "It ends here, never to be discussed again." I pierced Case with a look. "That means *everyone.*"

"Understood," Lockland said.

"No problem," Bender added.

"Fine by me," Case said as he began to swing his arm at the elbow, flexing his fist open and shut, turning it sideways as he made a show of examining it.

"Why are you doing that?" I asked, perturbed, knowing he was deliberately messing with me.

"The feeling only came back recently. I'm just making sure it still works."

Chapter 25

"Cozzi, you were a damn fool," I proclaimed, hand over my heart. "But I loved you all the same. You were like a grandfather to me on those few occasions our paths crossed. I'm sorry our time was cut short. Peace be with you." I'd never met my own grandfather. I could only imagine that if he'd still been alive, he would've been like Cozzi—a character with a story to tell and a kind heart.

That narrative, of course, would be ignoring every story my mother ever told me about her father, who had been a hard-ass militia man with little time for family. But there was always my father's father. I'd never met my dad, who died in a salvaging accident before I was born, but I was told he'd had a kind heart. Maybe he got it from his father?

I'd like to believe that.

We were all assembled at the edge of a blown-out building in the canals, minus Claire, who'd gone back to her job so as not to raise any suspicion. We'd ventured to one of the most deserted places we could find, where the buildings had been sheared off only meters from the sea, near the mouth of the harbor that would hopefully, eventually, carry Cozzi out to sea. Just like he wanted.

The old man was wrapped in another, bigger, burial shroud, not even a tuft of his white hair peeking through. My heart clenched. Losing people was inevitable in this unforgiving city, but that didn't make it hurt any less.

Lockland stood next to me. "Sir, you were a vital piece of this city. We are sad to see you go. May your soul pass on to a better place."

A short silence followed before Bender growled, "You were a nuisance, old man. Always getting in the way. Always asking for handouts." I shot him a glare before he continued, "But I wouldn't have had it any other way. You might outlive us all yet. I hope the sea serves you well." He finished with a three-finger salute.

I elbowed Darby, who was on my other side. He cleared his throat. "I didn't know you very well. You were nice…enough." I elbowed him again. "What?" He turned to me, exclaiming, "The man barely tolerated me! Every time he saw me, he called me a 'goofy brainiac with the overly large eyes,' whatever that meant. Then he barked at me until I left. Like, a real animal sound with growls and everything."

"Well," I said, stifling a laugh, "if you don't know what he meant, you're not such a brainiac after all."

"I know what brainiac means." He hesitated. "At least…I think I do. It's kind of an old-fashioned word."

Bender tipped his head back and snorted. "It means you have a big brain and you're smart. Even I know that. Nothing more, nothing less, *brainiac.*"

"Well," Darby huffed, "I am. But the way he always said it made it sound like an insult. Or a disease. How should I know?"

"Enough arguing," I said. "We're here to celebrate Cozzi's life and give him a decent sendoff." I nodded to Daze, who stood just in front of me. "Have anything to say, kid?"

Daze placed his right hand over his heart and glanced solemnly down at the shroud, which we'd strapped to a raft of dead branches. "You were a brave man, even though I never met you. Thank you for helping Holly. If you hadn't, I wouldn't be here." His words were heartfelt, and I gripped his shoulders, giving them a small squeeze.

Then I gave a side-eye to my left, where Case stood just behind Lockland. "Anything to add?" I asked. He was here because he happened to have brought Daze back from a treatment in the medi-pod and stuck around to help build the raft.

Transporting Cozzi through a bunch of torn-up buildings, while lugging a bunch of branches haphazardly twined together hadn't been easy.

Surprisingly, Case bowed his head. "Rest in peace, old man. May the heavens look down upon you kindly and may the sun shine on you once again. Our destinies are unknown, but our legacies live on forever. You will be remembered."

Before I could comment, Lockland responded with, "Amen."

"Amen," Bender added.

"Amen," Daze followed.

Darby huffed out an, "Amen."

Everyone looked at me expectantly. "Okay, okay, amen. Jeez, talk about old-fashioned," I muttered. "Nobody worships anymore."

"Since Cozzi was old, he would've liked it." Daze glanced up at me, his helmet half slipping down the back of his head.

"Yeah, he would have." I reset the thing on his skull and turned to Case. "Those were nice words for a guy you didn't even know."

He shrugged, flipping down his visor. "I told you before, my second sustainer family were Sun Optimists. They did a lot of praying to the obscured yellow disk in the sky. I picked up a couple of things. It seemed appropriate." He turned and walked away.

"It was," I murmured begrudgingly as I took out my Gem. I switched the level from high to low and aimed it at the foot of the raft, then nodded to Lockland. "Let him go."

Lockland poked the branches with a pole, and the old man drifted into the current. As the raft began to bob away, I pulled the trigger. The laser beamed out, catching the edge of the burial shroud.

Flames erupted.

We all watched as the raft bumped its way along the canal, almost getting hung up before catching the current once again. "It kind of reminds me of Cozzi shuffling down the street," I said, smiling. "Maybe he's guiding it cosmically."

"Or maybe he left this Earth a long-ass time ago," Bender said, turning to head out. "And doesn't give a fuck where that thing goes." Once we were back under the coverage of the building, he addressed the group. "We meet at my place in forty-eight hours. You guys need to be packed and ready to go." He jabbed a finger between Case, who stood a few meters away, and myself. "And no more arguments. You need him to help you find what Darby needs. You won't be able to do it on your own, so quit complaining."

"I'm not a child," I argued, trying hard not to sound like a child. "I can complete a mission by myself."

"Maybe, maybe not," Lockland said. "You're not familiar with the South or the sea, and he is. It makes sense that you two go together. We all have a job to do if you want to save Mary. If not"—he shrugged—"we can call the whole operation off. It's your decision."

"Why is it my call?" My mission was to head South in search of the sodium alginate in the form of seaweed. None of us was sure it still existed, but since it'd been likely Tandor had been the one to procure it in the first place, we were starting with his first known location.

Case had been assigned to help me, and I, being my naturally magnanimous self, was having trouble not resenting it, even though rationally I knew it was the right thing to do. Case was familiar with the locations and places Tandor and his group had been. Trying to find those on my own would take time—possibly longer than Mary had.

Lockland gave me a look, one that meant I should know better. "You're in charge of this entire thing. You were the one infected and the one who cares the most. If you call it off, we stay."

He was right. I did care the most, and I'd sworn to help Mary no matter what it took. "It's on," I said solemnly. "We'll be ready in forty-eight."

Darby stood off to the side. "Good, now that that's all cleared up, I'm heading back to the Emporium to get some work done." We'd moved his lab—the one he'd shared with the unaccounted-for Marta—to the Emporium because it held more space, and that's where Mary was.

Over the last few days, she'd been coherent, in and out of consciousness, but her condition had degraded severely over the last twelve hours, making this mission even more imperative.

"Daze and I'll go with you," I told him. I'd left Luce there. The Emporium was a little more than half a kilometer from here. It also wasn't too far from my residence in the canals, which I'd gone back to yesterday. To my great and total relief, nobody had infiltrated it, and it didn't seem that the government had any knowledge of the location.

We picked our way through the building and emerged onto the street. The guys headed to their crafts, which were waiting a short distance away. As Case left, I called, "We're taking *my* craft South. I'll get her to the barracks soon so we can pack her up."

His eyes pierced mine, even from a distance, as he slowly shook his head, bracing one arm on Seven. "We've already had this discussion. We need speed and room. Your craft has neither."

"Luce has the best tech available if we run into trouble. I'm not going to compromise safety," I tossed back.

"I'll modify his craft," Bender butted in. Before I could say any more, he held up a beefy hand. "Speed and tech win." Then he got in and shut the door, starting up his G5. Case slid into Seven next, likely to follow Bender back to the shop.

"Traitors," I mumbled.

"It won't be so bad going with Case," Daze assured me as we began to walk toward the Emporium, the rain pelting down harder than usual. "Seven is fast, and we need to take a lot of supplies."

Daze was excited for the trip. He, like most of us, had never ventured farther than a few kilometers from the city. I'd put him in charge of gathering food from the barracks, which he'd done with gusto. The piles were enormous. They could feed us for months. I still insisted that he spend time in the medi-pod, even though he looked and acted completely fine. He'd resisted at first, but was now resigned, knowing he wasn't going to win the argument, especially since I threatened to leave him home if he didn't comply.

Once inside the Emporium, a distinct sound came from Mary's room. It wasn't the usual noise of her trying to get free. It sounded like a voice.

Placing a finger to my lips, I drew my Gem. "Darby," I whispered as I moved ahead quietly, "you and Daze head to the lab. Let me handle this. If anything happens, go to Bender's."

He nodded.

I slipped into the hallway, my back against the wall, creeping slowly. Once I got to Mary's room, I took a deep breath before I lunged through the doorway.

Seeing the man next to her platform was shocking. He started, turning as he raised his hands.

"Ned?" I slowly lowered my weapon.

He kept his hands up. "No one was here," he stammered. "I…I knocked first. After Dill made me trap you, I slipped out as soon as I could. I never wanted to be part of this. I swear."

I hadn't given him much thought. A lot of Hutch's guys had gone down while I'd been out of my mind on Plush. Ned had been easy to overlook.

"Why are you here?" I wasn't ready to holster my weapon just yet.

"The gossip on the street is that you guys took out Hutch and Slim. I had to come and see for myself." His head turned slightly toward the bed, his expression full of anguish. "It's my fault Mary was taken. She was my neighbor and friend. Dill took a liking to her, and before I knew it, he'd made her his first Plushie." His remorse was front and center. "I would've never introduced them had I known." Mary began to moan. Ned's longish hair fell in his face as he leaned forward, tentatively touching her arm. "Can you help her?"

I holstered my Gem and took a step forward. Behind me, Daze had taken a position to cover me, his taser out. Our symbiotic relationship was coming along nicely. I gave a nod of thanks to the kid as I moved farther into the room.

"We're going to try," I said, reaching the edge of the platform. "You can facilitate that by telling me everything you know about Hutch's operations. Was this his only headquarters? What about Marta? My friend Darby worked with her. She's a scientist, but we haven't been able to track her down, and we have no idea if she's alive. She likely has knowledge about the cure."

"I've never heard of a Marta, I'm sorry. But I hadn't been a 'recruit' for very long. They kept most of us in the dark about specifics. I can take you to Dill's place, though. I don't think you'll find much, but it might be worth a try."

I nodded. "That would be helpful."

He glanced down at Mary. "Is she conscious? Can she hear me?"

"I'm not sure," I answered truthfully. "She could last night, but she's getting increasingly worse by the hour. We're doing everything we can, but we're extremely short on time."

He bowed his head. "I understand. We can leave for Dill's shortly."

I turned to give him some privacy with his friend. It was obvious he was remorseful about what had happened. Forgiving him wasn't on the agenda yet, but if he could provide us with necessary information, we'd see.

Daze holstered his taser as we walked out. I'd confiscated the laser gun Bender had given him when they'd busted in here, promising that I would give it back once I had time to train him. Having that thing go off accidentally could kill someone, and it wasn't going to be me or him.

Once we were in the hallway, Daze asked, "Do you think that guy's telling the truth? Was he Mary's friend?"

"I'm not sure," I said. "But based on our earlier interactions, I'm going to give him the benefit of the doubt."

"If he hurts Mary, he's going to get a taste of pain."

My eyebrows rose. "Oh, yeah?"

"Definitely." He nodded. "Nobody messes with us and gets away with it." His voice was full of bravado.

I chuckled. "That's for sure." I mussed his hair because I could. "Now let's go find Darby. I need some info before we head out. After we check out Dill's place, we have a lot of packing to do."

In the lab, Darby was hunched over the pico, as usual. He didn't look up. He likely didn't even know Daze had left.

"I just ran into one of Hutch's recruits. He was in with Mary," I told him. "His name is Ned, and he's harmless. He's going to take us to Dill's residence. I'm hoping we can start putting the pieces together about what happened to Marta and maybe get a lead on where Slim called home. It seems Slim was in charge of procuring or making the Plush. From what Claire told us, he very well could've been in contact with that secret group in the government, the Bureau of Truth."

Darby nodded absentmindedly. "That's good. Very good." He pointed at the screen. "See here, this formula is contradictory. In the actual data, it says one thing, but in the language of code, it specifies something entirely different." He looked up, meeting my gaze for the first time. His eyes were bloodshot. He probably hadn't slept more than an hour or two. "Why would they do that?"

I pulled a chair over and sat as Daze leaned against the table next to us. "I don't know, Darb. Maybe someone was trying to cover something up? When folks started having bad reactions to Plush, I bet there was a lot of fallout and people were scurrying around trying to avoid blame. Lives were getting ruined."

"Yeah, maybe," he said, though his tone remained unconvinced. "Or maybe they deleted all the damning evidence, but forgot to wipe the formulas. That seems more likely." He straightened. "Thank goodness for the audiobooks I found over the years, or I'd have never been able to read these. I procured one that discussed bio-engineering when I was about thirteen.

It was all about elemental compounds, and it was one of the only things I had to listen to as a kid. I guess it paid off."

"I'll say. We're damn lucky. Without you, this wouldn't be possible," I said earnestly. "Before we go, I need you to level with me." That got his attention. He cocked his head toward me. "How likely is the success of this mission? Do you actually think once we're back you'll be able to figure out a cure if we gather all the ingredients you need?" He was running low on a few things, but we had no idea where to procure them. Guesses were all we had.

His eyes focused somewhere over my head. "I'd like to say it's fifty-fifty," he answered. "But in reality, it's probably about twenty percent, and that's being generous."

"But it worked on me," I pointed out. "That gives me hope."

He nodded. "That's true, but you were infected for less than a day and a half. We're talking about curing people who have been ingesting Plush for years on end. If everything documented in the formulas is correct"—he glanced down at the pico, then back at me—"it could work. But we're going to need a mass supply of it to help everyone."

I nodded as I stood. "Twenty percent is good enough for me. Mary's only been infected for a week or two. Her chances of coming out of this are better, right?"

"Again, hard to know, but based on what we've seen

with you, I'd say the odds are in favor of her making a full recovery."

I walked to the door, Daze trailing after me. I turned at the last minute. "And, Darby, stay out of trouble while I'm gone. We need you in one piece."

"That's the plan. That's always the plan."

As we headed out, I slung my arm across Daze's shoulders. "This journey isn't going to be easy, kid."

"I know. But it doesn't scare me." His voice held a note of something that belied his words.

"Then what does?" We stopped in front of Mary's door. I nodded to Ned, and he followed us out.

"Losing you."

I dunked his head playfully. "That's not going to happen. I'm tough, if you haven't noticed. You're stuck with me for the duration."

"Does that mean you're going to sustainer me for longer than a year?" His voice held hope.

"Don't get ahead of yourself, kid. One day at a time."

DANGER'S RACE

A HOLLY DANGER NOVEL: BOOK THREE

AMANDA CARLSON

Chapter 1

"Can we trust this Ned guy?" Bender asked, his voice expressing more than a little grumble. It was just after dawn, and an early riser he wasn't. But the timing couldn't be helped. We were gathered in his shop, the communal place for most of our meetings, to discuss our new mission. We were each taking off in separate directions to find key ingredients Darby needed to concoct a cure for Plush, the pharma-psychotic drug that permanently altered the DNA of the user, turning them into mindless pleasure seekers.

It was the best—and likely only—chance we had to help Mary, an innocent woman who'd been caught up in the dangerous games of zealots and outskirts in this dark city. Mary was the first in a long line of seekers who needed our help. But starting with her made sense. She'd been recently infected and had a high chance of pulling through with no lasting effects.

I stood with my back against the wall, arms crossed. Daze sat in a chair, fiddling with a gadget he'd found on one of the worktables. Lockland had his shoulder braced against the cooling unit, and Bender was situated on his regular stool, a jug of aminos gripped in his fist.

Case stood off to the side, near the hallway we'd just come through. It was strange to have him here, but since he was my partner on this journey, it was necessary. Darby was back at the Emporium, with Ned, the person who was currently in question, trying to finalize everything so when we arrived back with all the necessary ingredients—hopefully within a few days—he could put the cure together.

"All I can go by is our history together," I told the group. "When I first met him, he wanted to make a deal. He wasn't in Hutch's group by choice. Then, two days ago, the day we sent Cozzi off, he took me to Dill's residence and we scoured the place. It was a dump. I'm pretty sure the cockroaches still scurrying around the city have better accommodations. Dill, it seems, was a fairly new recruit to the group and not in the know. Ned was friends with Mary before she was infected, and wants to help." I shrugged. "He's agreed to protect Darby and take care of Mary while we're gone. Claire can't get away, and the rest of us are taking off to places unknown. He's trustworthy enough on a non-vital level, but I'll go with whatever we decide. He'll walk without issue if we tell him to."

"Ned can stay," Lockland said, shoving off from the cooling unit as he reached into his pocket, withdrawing a small box. "Having somebody look after Mary sounds like a good idea to me." He walked over and placed the item into my now outstretched hand.

"What's this?" I asked, as I popped the top off, leaning over to examine it, not believing my eyes. In the box, nestled between a piece of soft cloth, sat a very rare status reader. "No way! Where did you find this?"

I knew what it was based on its shape and color. It was a small oval made of white, semi-shiny polymer. These were fairly common before the dark days. It had a flat section on the bottom so it could rest on a counter or a desktop. They were purported to relay directional information, temperature, atmospheric readings, and could even detect human matter, all upon request. People called them "status eggs" for short. I only had a picture to go on, but it did look remarkably like an egg.

I'd actually found one intact a long time ago, but hadn't been able to get it to work. Most of the time they were smashed or damaged beyond repair.

Daze hustled to my side, intrigued by what I held in my hand. He made a move to touch it, but I shook my head, pulling my hand back. "There's a reason it's in this box with the cloth," I told him. "The organic matter on your fingers could contaminate the sensors. It uses Lidar technology to measure distances and take readings." Lidar was short for Light Detection and Ranging. According to the data, the egg sent out light out to accurately detect things. "When they were first made, they had some sort of coating on them, but who knows if it's worn off or not. Let's not take any chances." I glanced at Lockland. "Does the voice activation work or is this one manual only?" It had a switch tucked inside the flat bottom that would turn on the basic settings so they would be displayed on the top of the shell. Voice activation, as a whole, hadn't held up over the years. The software needed to generate it was fragile and decayed over time.

Lockland arched a cagey eyebrow at me. "Give it a try. To power it up, say 'reader on'."

I'd lowered the box in front of Daze. "Go ahead, you try first."

"What should I ask it to do?"

I shrugged. "I don't know. Ask it what the temperature is or how many of us are in the room."

"Okay." Daze licked his lips like he was getting ready for a long, important oration. I grinned as he cleared his throat and, in a voice several decibels lower than his natural speaking voice, commanded, "Reader on."

Amazingly, the thing popped to life.

An array of colors dotted the surface, tiny pinpricks of light blinking faster than I could track—the Lidar tech in action.

Everybody gathered around to see this rare piece of technology actually work, including Case.

"Who needs to know the damn temperature?" Bender grumbled. "It's always cold and rainy. End of story." His attitude belied the fact that his eyes were riveted on the thing, just like everybody else's.

A few low beeps issued out as the colored lights jumped around on the surface before solidifying into two glowing green numerals. The number fifteen flashed twice, followed by a soft, fluid female voice, "The temperature is fifteen degrees Celsius, the barometer is dropping rapidly, expect rain."

She'd answered Bender's question—that hadn't really been a question—with a real answer. It was nothing short of amazing.

"Expect?" Bender snorted. "How about it's raining now."

"Stop spoiling the fun, fun-spoiler," I told him as I nudged Daze. "Go ahead, ask it something else."

"Um," Daze hedged. Then in the same low, comical baritone, he asked, his lips only centimeters from the thing, "How many people are in the room?"

The egg's lights zoomed around on the surface, shooting off a kaleidoscope of colors. Several beeps sounded and the number five flashed again. After a second, the woman's voice, which was kind of freaking me out because it was so polished and perfect, flowed out, "I detect five humans within two meters, nine humans within twenty meters, and thirty-four humans, and several invertebrates, within one hundred meters."

We all gasped.

Holy shit.

DANGER'S RACE is available now! Don't miss out on the further adventures of Holly & her crew.

NOTHING IS CREATED WITHOUT A GREAT TEAM.

My thanks to:

Awesome Cover design: Damonza.com

Digital and print formatting: Author E.M.S

Copyedits/proofs: Joyce Lamb

Final proof: Marlene Engel

ABOUT THE AUTHOR

Amanda Carlson is a graduate of the University of Minnesota, with a BA in both Speech and Hearing Science & Child Development. She went on to get an A.A.S in Sign Language Interpreting and worked as an interpreter until her first child was born. She's the author of the high octane Jessica McClain urban fantasy series published by Orbit, the Sin City Collectors paranormal romance series, the contemporary fantasy Phoebe Meadows series, and the futuristic/dystopian Holly Danger series. Look for these books in stores everywhere. She lives in Minneapolis with her husband and three kids.

Find her all over social media

Website: amandacarlson.com
Facebook: facebook.com/authoramandacarlson
Twitter: @amandaccarlson
Instagram: @author_amanda